Old School
Albert Smith's Mystery Thrillers Book 2
Steve Higgs

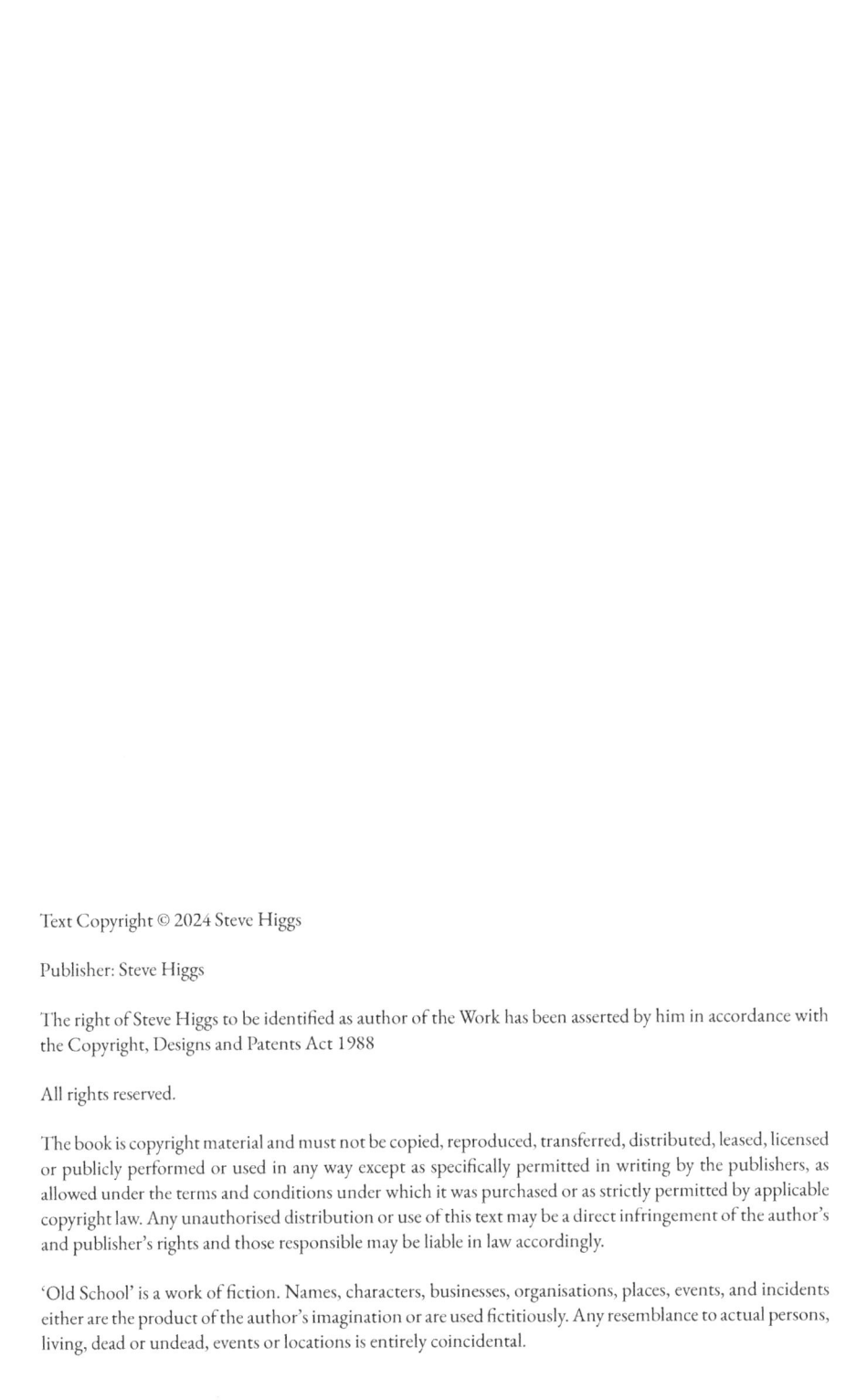

Text Copyright © 2024 Steve Higgs

Publisher: Steve Higgs

The right of Steve Higgs to be identified as author of the Work has been asserted by him in accordance with the Copyright, Designs and Patents Act 1988

All rights reserved.

The book is copyright material and must not be copied, reproduced, transferred, distributed, leased, licensed or publicly performed or used in any way except as specifically permitted in writing by the publishers, as allowed under the terms and conditions under which it was purchased or as strictly permitted by applicable copyright law. Any unauthorised distribution or use of this text may be a direct infringement of the author's and publisher's rights and those responsible may be liable in law accordingly.

'Old School' is a work of fiction. Names, characters, businesses, organisations, places, events, and incidents either are the product of the author's imagination or are used fictitiously. Any resemblance to actual persons, living, dead or undead, events or locations is entirely coincidental.

Contents

1. Prologue – The Crime   1
2. Chapter 1   3
3. Chapter 2   7
4. Chapter 3   9
5. Chapter 4   11
6. Chapter 5   15
7. Chapter 6   20
8. Chapter 7   22
9. Chapter 8   28
10. Chapter 9   30
11. Chapter 10   34
12. Chapter 11   39
13. Chapter 12   42
14. Chapter 13   45
15. Chapter 14   49
16. Chapter 15   54
17. Chapter 16   61
18. Chapter 17   65

19.	Chapter 18	69
20.	Chapter 19	76
21.	Chapter 20	78
22.	Chapter 21	85
23.	Chapter 22	90
24.	Chapter 23	94
25.	Chapter 24	100
26.	Chapter 25	102
27.	Chapter 26	105
28.	Chapter 27	109
29.	Chapter 28	116
30.	Chapter 29	122
31.	Chapter 30	129
32.	Chapter 31	132
33.	Chapter 32	138
34.	Chapter 33	141
35.	Chapter 34	147
36.	Chapter 35	149
37.	Chapter 36	150
38.	Chapter 37	155
39.	Chapter 38	157
40.	Chapter 39	162
41.	Chapter 40	164
42.	Chapter 41	166

43.	Chapter 42	170
44.	Chapter 43	172
45.	Chapter 44	174
46.	Chapter 45	176
47.	Chapter 46	177
48.	Chapter 47	179
49.	Chapter 48	182
50.	Chapter 49	184
51.	Chapter 50	187
52.	Chapter 51	191
53.	Chapter 52	193
54.	Chapter 53	195
55.	Chapter 54	196
56.	Chapter 55	198
57.	Chapter 56	202
58.	Author's Notes:	207
59.	History of the Dish	209
60.	Recipe	211
61.	What's Next for Albert and Rex?	214
62.	Free Books and More	216

Prologue – The Crime

The rain, as though choosing to punish them for their wickedness, continued to batter down. They were already drenched, the umbrellas they brought along abandoned when the weather's determined efforts defeated any attempt to stay dry.

It had taken more than an hour to get the hole deep enough. Deep enough to hide a body. It wasn't lowered gently into the hole, there were no prayers or words of remembrance said, and only one person shed any tears.

Not that they could be seen among the raindrops.

When the hole was finally filled in, the ground around it a quagmire of slick mud, the rain was employed to hide the footprints their efforts left behind.

The field in which they dug the shallow grave sat on a patch of high ground above the village. No one would ever excavate it. Drucker's Field was publicly owned land designated part of an area of outstanding natural beauty, so there was no danger it would be sold off to be planted with crops or developed for housing. In the spring the wildflowers would grow again and the people trudging back to their homes in the middle of the night had already assigned two of their number to reseed the scar their efforts would leave.

A story had to be concocted and arrangements made, but they were confident few questions would be asked. The eight of them, all of a similar age, felt no sense of triumph in what they had just done. Justice perhaps, but certainly no joy. They would each have picked a different outcome, but they had to play the hand they were dealt, and all agreed this was the best solution.

The dead person would not be missed, and though there might be a few questions, it was unlikely anyone would challenge the version of events the group would spread through the village. They would whisper their rumour here and there … 'Did you hear about … just up and left in the night …' and there would be no evidence to suggest it was anything but the truth.

And should someone feel the need to delve a little deeper, well, they had the law quite literally on their side.

Chapter 1

"What do you think, Rex?" Albert turned his face upward and sniffed the mountain air.

Rex was doing the same, his muzzle raised high to capture whatever scents the breeze might contain.

They were in La Obrey, a small village in the Alsace region of France, famous for being the birthplace of the world-famous bretzel. Like many well-known dishes, the village's claim was contested by a dozen other sites across France and it remained entirely possible the truth of the dish's origins could be traced to an Austrian baker.

Arriving by train the previous evening, Albert's pilgrimage to sample and savour the dish at its source was as much about avoiding his home as it was anything else. Left alone when his wife passed, her presence permeated the very air inside their house and though he didn't believe in ghosts, he was constantly haunted by her memory.

At seventy-eight, he had accepted that he was no longer a young man. By the same token, he didn't think he was old either. Old was when you hit ninety-five. He had a long way to go to get to that point.

A former police detective superintendent, he had recently exposed a shocking spate of crimes perpetrated by and on behalf of a distant member of the royal family. The very public nature of the enquiry that followed was another reason behind his decision to be elsewhere. In France the story of the British aristocrat and the pensioner who took him down was known, but he wasn't being recognised every five minutes like he was in England.

Relaxing on a bench with a quietly babbling stream trickling away to his right, it was a little too cool to be outside. Yet all the locals commented on how unseasonably warm it was. Well, all except those who said it ought to already be snowing.

Regardless of the temperature, Albert elected to eat his regional delicacy with a view of the mountains backdropping the picturesque village. Celeste, the landlady of his delightful guesthouse, recommended a walking route that took him to a high point just above the village.

It was a bit of a trek, she admitted, but worth it for the view. Knowing Rex would appreciate a good walk, and telling himself this was what would keep his own body moving, Albert found the cut through between the houses – it was right where Celeste said it would be.

A bit of a trek proved to be accurate, but Albert was resigned to a few days of walking hills. Drawn by the promise of incredible views, the guesthouse in which they were staying sat at the highest part of the village. The views were as claimed, but to get to anywhere else in the village was a mission.

From inside his coat, where they'd retained most of their freshly baked warmth, he produced a brown paper bag. It contained three bretzels, grease staining the brown paper.

Rex hadn't taken his eyes off the bag since his human came out of the shop carrying it. His world was filled with glorious smells, his powerful olfactory system able to sift, sort, categorise, and store each for later retrieval. Everything, from the scent of a car's exhaust to the odour of squirrel poop could be recalled and compared at a moment's notice. However, it was food smells that dominated his canine brain.

Big for a German Shepherd, he had trained as a police dog before being fired from the role after only a few months. His handlers deemed him to be unworkable, but Rex knew the real reason he lost his job: they couldn't keep up with him.

Blessed with an unusually perceptive mind, Rex had thought of himself as a detective. He could smell the clues and believed it was his job to track the criminals. His handlers wanted him to bark at people and occasionally sniff his way to find a person. It was all so pedestrian when he was capable of so much more.

Of course, at that precise moment, the only thing he wanted to detect was the inside of his human's brown paper bag.

"*Are you going to open that, or what?*" he nudged Albert's leg.

Albert, quite used to his dog's strange whining and chuffing noises, guessed what he was trying to impart.

He had the bag under his nose, drinking in the heavenly scent of warm bread, but the contents would turn cold soon so it was time to devour.

Extracting the first, he broke it into two pieces.

"Now, don't snatch, thank you, Rex," he warned, handing a piece to his dog.

Rex took it gently enough, but rolled it across his tongue and swallowed without chewing.

Albert rolled his eyes. "That's no way to savour your food, Rex." As if to demonstrate how it should be done, he bit into his half, closing his eyes when the delicate morsel melted into his tongue.

He was about to take a second bite when a shout caught his attention. It came from his left and originated from somewhere beyond a line of trees.

Rex heard the shout too but chose to ignore it. His attention was on the hunk of bretzel held loosely between his human's fingers.

The shout rang out and was fading away, but there was no mistaking the panic and horror it contained.

Twisting on the bench to get a better look, Albert squinted at the distant trees. Until he felt a slight tug on his fingers, that is.

Rex, well aware of the correct protocol, could only do so much to control himself when his human placed a tasty treat so close to his face.

Glaring down at his now empty hand and Rex's crumb covered jowls, he narrowed his eyes.

"Seriously, Rex? That was my half."

"*It was jolly tasty,*" Rex replied. Then hopefully, he added, "*Is there any more?*"

Gripping the bag and the two remaining bretzels a little tighter, Albert used his free hand to push himself up off the bench.

The shout hadn't been followed by a second and the mountain air was back to its tranquil, quietness.

Staring at the direction from which it came, Albert skewed his lips to one side in thought. There was no one else around. In fact, he considered it possible that no one else had even heard the scream. They were a hundred yards from the nearest of the houses, and the woods were a farther hundred yards in the opposite direction – too far for the residents to have heard it.

Muttering under his breath, for choosing to investigate and finding himself embroiled in a murderous mystery was the last thing he should be doing, Albert clicked his tongue to let Rex know they were moving, and started toward the trees.

Chapter 2

Rex trotted along gamely at his human's side. Off the lead, as he would expect to be in the countryside, Rex saw little reason to stray. One of his primary roles in life was to protect the old man he lived with. They had become as close as a man and a dog could get during the previous adventure, not that Rex conceived it as such.

They went places, that was what he liked, and no two days were the same. There was always something tasty to eat, and everywhere they went the air was different and filled with wonderous new scents.

However, if his human had one major failing, ignoring his deplorably terrible sense of smell, it was that he currently held a bag of food that he was supposed to be sharing.

"*Oi*," barked Rex, getting in front of Albert. "*Aren't you forgetting something?*"

Misinterpreting his dog's behaviour – another weakness that constantly irked Rex – Albert said, "I just want to see what that shout was about. There might be someone in trouble."

Able to understand a good portion of what the humans around him said, Rex picked up on the key word 'trouble' and forgot about the bretzels, if only for a second.

"*Trouble?*" he sniffed the air and his pupils dilated instantly. Certain it had to be his preoccupation with the warm bread products that stopped him from noticing the coppery tang of blood in the air, Rex leaned into the scent now. It was coming from dead ahead, the direction his human was going.

Impressed by the old man, Rex reminded himself that while smell was unarguably the strongest and most accurate sense available, humans were known to use sight and hearing with great effectiveness at times.

He ran ahead a little, his nose up to track the scent when a check of the ground confirmed there was nothing to find other than some rabbit droppings.

Albert called, "Rex!" not wanting him to get too far ahead. The walk up the hill had been taxing even though he'd taken it slow. He might not have attempted it at all had Celeste not claimed she did it at least once a week. He wasn't about to ask the lady her age, but she had to be well into her eighties.

Getting closer to the trees, Albert heard a voice filtering through. Straining to hear, he assessed that it was one person only – a young woman, he believed. She was jabbering excitedly in French and struggling to get her words out such was the emotion packed into them. That she kept pausing between blurted sentences made Albert believe she was on the phone.

His French might once have been passable, but the last time he used it had to be more than twenty years ago and he was struggling to make out anything the young woman was saying.

Calling Rex back, Albert clipped a lead to his collar, and reaching the trees, he called out to announce his presence.

"Hellooo?" he tried to sound friendly and harmless. "Hellooo? I heard shouting. Is everything all right?"

The voice stopped abruptly, and when Albert rounded the next tree, he caught sight of the woman he could hear.

In dark trousers over walking boots, she was easy to spot for the bright red Northface coat she wore. Her dark brown hair was pulled roughly into a ponytail, and she wore glasses but no makeup.

Startled to see Albert approaching, she yelled in panic into the phone she held and this time Albert understood what she said.

"Come quickly! I think the killer has returned!"

Chapter 3

Unable to react fast enough, Albert was just starting to raise his hands to show they were empty, when the woman pulled out a knife. Fumbling her phone, she dropped and tried to catch it before choosing the knife as the more important thing to hold.

Her hands were shaking uncontrollably, so the knife, a six-inch thing she'd produced from a sheath on her belt, wobbled unconvincingly in the air at arm's length.

Rex's top lip curled back. He could tell the woman was scared, but she was holding a weapon and that made her a problem he needed to deal with. Taking a determined step forward, he was getting ready to launch himself forward when Albert pulled him back.

"No, Rex. No chase and bite."

Rex relaxed his muscles, but did not completely stand down. He was poised, ready to react at the first sign the woman with the knife meant to harm his human.

"Hello," Albert tried again, "I'm afraid my French isn't up to much. Can you speak English?"

The woman replied by saying in perfect English, "I have called the police!"

Albert nodded. "Jolly good. Are you okay though? I heard a shout." She had also referred to him as 'the killer' which suggested there was something more to the young woman's story than was currently apparent. He noted but did not remark on her accent. There was something off about it as though French was not her first language and nor was English.

"Who are you?" the woman demanded, the knife still wavering in the air.

"I'm Albert and this is Rex." He cast his eyes down to her phone. Whoever was on the other end was still trying to continue their conversation. "We are tourists staying in La Obrey." He held up the brown bag from the bakery as if that served as proof. "Is that the police?" he asked. "You can pick it up if you wish. I'm not going to do anything to hurt you."

Having come through the trees, Albert found himself standing at the edge of a field. It angled downward to his left, gently curving like a pillow until it reached more trees. The grass had been left to grow into meadowland, but where towering strands must have grown tall in the summer, they were dead now.

However, it wasn't so much the field that Albert noticed, but the excavations that dominated this part of it. A series of trenches, each a few feet deep, had been dug into the soil, the spoil carefully arranged on tarpaulins. They were marked with little flags of varying colours and Albert believed he knew what he was looking at: an archaeological dig.

When the young woman failed to reach for her phone and the voice at the other end became yet more urgent, he proposed a new strategy. "I tell you what. I'll turn around. Will that help?"

Albert shuffled his feet until he was facing back into the trees and waited a few seconds, hoping to be rewarded with the sound of the woman resuming her phone conversation.

When she began to jabber, Albert slowly turned to face her once more. She still held the knife, but now her left hand was holding the phone to her ear and she looked a little less petrified than she had.

Throwing caution to the wind, Albert chose to take a closer look at the excavations. Just as he expected, he only needed to get a few feet closer to catch sight of a boot sticking up at an unnatural angle. There was a man lying in one of the ditches.

He was very clearly dead.

Chapter 4

The woman backed away as he came closer, still talking to the police, Albert assumed. He didn't want to interfere with the body or ruin any evidence that might be present in the immediate vicinity of the body, but he was curious to see what might have killed the man.

Selecting a better angle, Albert was able to see his face.

Rex, meanwhile, sampled the air. It was loaded with the heavy scent of blood, but filtering that out he found the man's aftershave and deodorant, the wax on his walking boots to make them water repellent, and the product in his hair. The woman also carried a unique blend of scents which he stored away for future reference.

Albert crouched a little, a position from which his knees and thighs would protest when it was time to rise again. The victim – Albert already doubted the death was accidental – had been struck on the skull. There was significant blood loss from his hairline, but no other injury Albert could see. The blood had soaked into the man's shoulder-length blonde hair where it matted and dried. Combined with his pallor, Albert judged the murder to have occurred the previous evening.

A bulge in the back right pocket of his jeans showed his wallet remained. Albert acknowledged that the contents could have been emptied, so robbery could still have been the motive, but he doubted it. In general, thieves do not replace wallets once they have taken them, and in an increasingly cashless world it seemed unlikely the man would have a worthwhile enough amount of money to steal.

The woman finished her phone conversation, but didn't hang up the call. She was frightened and wanted the comfort of a person at the other end of the phone.

Using both hands on his knees to regain his full height, Albert scratched at Rex's neck and gave him a pat on his shoulder.

"*You think maybe she killed him?*" Rex asked. Still sniffing the air, he wanted to get closer to the body. If the woman's scent was on it, or if it was not, either would tell a story.

Albert was about to ask the woman her name and try once again to reinforce the idea that he meant her no harm when a new voice echoed across the field.

"Julienne!"

The woman spun around, deflating with relief that someone she recognised was coming.

Albert had no need to remain where he was but knew with absolute confidence that the woman was going to describe him to the police the moment they arrived, and they would want to talk to him. It was simpler to just hang around and wait for them.

A man in his forties stormed across the field making a beeline for the woman. He wore glasses with a thick black rim and a trim black beard with grey coming in around his chin. His head bore almost no hair at all, and what remained at the back and sides had been shaved down to almost nothing.

Dressed for the cold, he wore a Timberwolf coat with a fur lined hood hanging down his back, hardwearing black trousers spattered with dirt and mud, and stout walking boots just like the woman and the poor man in the ditch.

"Lars!" Julienne shouted back. "It's Bjorn. He's ... he's ..." she couldn't get the last word out and now Albert realised why her French accent was so odd – she wasn't French. If pushed to guess, he would plumb for Swedish, but she could just as easily be Danish or from one of the other Scandinavian countries.

Lars covered the rest of the distance across the field, the red in his cheeks matching the look of concern in his eyes.

"What is going on? Why have you got that knife?" Lars glared accusingly at Albert.

Unable to answer, Julienne pointed to the ditch.

Albert watched when the breath caught in Lars' chest; his shock was genuine. He should have predicted it, but Albert was too slow with his shout of warning and could only watch when Lars jumped into the excavation.

"No, that's a crime scene!" he yelled. "You could be destroying vital evidence."

Lars reached for Bjorn, but his hands faltered before he touched the man, the sightless eyes enough to tell him there was no hope for resuscitation. Now staring up at Albert, he growled, "Did you do this?"

Seeing the man's aggressive face, Rex curled his top lip again, exposing his teeth to an accompanying growl of his own.

"No, Rex," Albert commanded. Meeting Lars' eyes, he said, "I heard the young lady's cry and came to see if she was all right, nothing more." He wanted to point out that killers returning to the scene of a crime is a terrible cliché to be reserved for bad films and worse books, but chose to let his calm demeanour speak for him.

"He's lying!" argued Julienne. "He has to be. No one would hurt Bjorn. Everyone loved him."

Albert drew in a deep breath. "You called the police, yes?"

Julienne opened her mouth to respond, but Lars got in first.

"You did what!"

"I called the police," Julienne replied, her voice carrying a tone that made her sound unsure and the reply came out sounding more like a question to check she had done the right thing.

Lars hung his head, then placed his hands on his hips and stared up at the sky as though asking God to explain.

"Your friend has been murdered," Albert pointed out. "The police need to be involved. Now can I please ask that you carefully step away from the body and touch as little as possible?"

Lars closed his eyes and gave a small shake of his head. To Albert it looked as if the man was fighting to come to terms with his new reality. He was upset, as one might expect, but Albert didn't believe it was Bjorn's death impacting his emotions.

It was something else instead.

Chapter 5

The police arrived ten minutes later, three squad cars followed by an unmarked car appearing at the edge of the field to the west where they parked behind a newish grey camper van. They unloaded gear from the boots of their cars, donning different footwear to traverse the soggy field. They carried two fold-out crates between them.

The first to arrive was a man in his mid-fifties. Recognising the insignia as that of a captain, the three solid bars indicating he'd held the rank for some years, Albert surmised he was likely the senior officer in the region.

His hair contained more grey than its original black though his moustache was fighting hard to resist the onslaught of middle age. His dark brown eyes studied the scene and people ahead as he approached, and he moved with an athletic ease. Lean and tall in a shape that would have been called 'beanpole' when Albert was younger, he looked like someone who spent many hours running in his leisure time. The man's face was dominated by what Albert mentally labelled as a Gallic nose. Worried such a term might be considered politically incorrect or just plain rude, he kept it to himself, but the man's nose was both large and bulbous.

Julienne's knife was back where it belonged in the sheath on her belt, the calming influence of Lars to thank for its disappearance. Both of them were standing off to one side some twenty yards from the ditch and their colleague's body. They had been joined by Peter, the fourth member of their team. He looked just as stunned as Julienne and could barely take his eyes from the terrible sight of their dead friend.

Albert hadn't learned much about them in the intervening period accept that they hailed from a Swedish museum and were in La Obrey to dig for evidence of a Stone Age settlement.

He then overheard that they had been celebrating Julienne's birthday the previous evening - she had turned twenty-six – and had not seen Bjorn since. He was rostered to watch over the dig site last night, sleeping in the camper van parked at the western edge of the field.

Albert thought the need to watch a bunch of ditches at night to be questionable, but assumed it was nothing more than the archaeologists taking their work seriously.

It was past breakfast time and Julienne had been coming to start her day when she found Bjorn's body lying in one of their excavations.

"And you are?" the chief of police enquired. He'd introduced himself to Albert as Captaine de police Allard. Albert had quietly observed the man working, showing his experience and maturity by calmly directing the actions of his team while establishing that he was very much in charge and the civilians needed to treat him as such.

Albert gave his name, breathing a sigh of relief when it wasn't instantly recognised. His statement was taken and he gave them the address of the bed and breakfast where he was staying in La Obrey. Since he didn't have much to say and the police could see no evidence to suggest he was anything other than the passing tourist he claimed to be, they sent him on his way.

However, when he turned to go, Rex held fast.

His overactive nose had picked up on something unexpected.

"Come along, Rex," Albert gave a gentle tug on the lead. "There's no reason to stay here any longer and we shall become quite unwelcome if we linger."

Rex didn't budge. In fact, he leaned into his collar pulling to go in the opposite direction, back toward the excavations.

"*I just need to get closer,*" he whined. "*You'll understand if you just let me show you.*"

"No, Rex. We have to go." Albert reeled in the lead, taking himself closer to Rex rather than trying to pull his dog away.

Rex dug in with his paws, but when his human planted his feet either side of his ribs and hooked a hand through his collar, he knew the only options were to accept defeat or choose to really fight. The latter would not see an increase in his biscuit ration and could result in Albert getting hurt.

Reluctantly, he turned from the ditches, but even being led away before he could properly investigate, he was convinced about the nature of the scent he detected. It was below the ground still but there was no mistaking the odour of a dead human.

There was a second body not far from the first.

Guiding Rex back through the trees that would lead them back to their accommodation, Albert spotted someone. They shifted position and it was their movement that caught Albert's eye.

Forty yards away at the edge of the trees, someone was trying to be invisible. Hiding behind a tree that wasn't quite wide enough to provide the cover they required, they bolted when Albert stared right at the spot in which they hid.

Now they were in the open Albert could see it was a man. He wasn't old; his body able to burst into action, but despite the thick winter coat, Albert got the impression he was looking at someone middle aged or older – sixties perhaps. They didn't have the sprightliness of youth, and a thickening around the core suggested the spread so often associated with one's metabolism slowing down.

It was hard to judge his height, and Albert only saw the back of the man's head as he ran away mostly hidden by the trees. He had sandy hair and was probably around six feet in height. As descriptions go it wasn't a lot to go on. The only other element to record was his coat. It was a dark green colour; a wise choice for a person trying to blend into the woodland. At the top of the right sleeve sat a round, silver patch. Albert believed he would recognise it if he saw it again.

Rex saw it too, his whole body tensing. Was his human about to set him loose. Rex loved playing chase with humans. They were so easy to catch that he could mess around and enjoy the game if he wanted.

Albert's right hand twitched, indecision stalling his movement. If he released Rex, his dog would catch the man in a few seconds, but would then tackle him to the ground and sink his teeth in. Even if Rex was sensible about it and didn't tear the man's flesh, a dog bite is a jolly painful thing.

Was the man sneakily watching the crime scene because he was the killer returning to the scene of the crime? The thought brought an ironic smile to his face – hadn't he only just considered that such concepts are silly clichés? Just as likely was that the man was curious, but chose to observe from a distance. Albert couldn't set Rex on him unless he was sure, so he did the next best thing; he tried to give chase himself.

Crashing through the trees, Albert knew from bitter experience that his knees would start to protest after only thirty or so seconds, and that if he pushed himself too hard he would be sore for days, every joint from his hips downward conspiring to punish his over exuberance.

Excited by the old man's burst of speed, Rex tried to run, nearly yanking Albert from his feet when his lead reached full stretch.

"*Come on!*" he barked. "*Let's get him! You can let me off, I won't bite him. I'll just ...*" Rex thought about what he could do instead. "*I'll round him up like a sheep dog. I'll be a human dog!*"

Albert lost sight of the man in the green coat almost instantly. There were too many trees between them, but nearing the edge of the small copse that bordered the field he caught sight of his quarry once more.

He wasn't trying to catch him though. More sort of catch up. If the man was anything other than another tourist out for a walk, Albert wanted to see his face and be able to identify him should the need arise.

However, breaking through the trees, both he and Rex could see the man properly and the person he was now looking at was not the one who ran away. He was coming toward them for a start.

He had sandy hair going grey, Albert observed, and was somewhere around sixty years of age, but he wore a metallic red winter jacket, the puffy kind that skiers favour. Unless he was some kind of quick-change expert, it was someone different.

Albert slowed his pace. The man in the green coat had moved faster than he'd expected, making it to the next set of trees where he was able to use them for cover. By now he would be at the top edge of the village and able to vanish.

Puffing slightly from his burst of speed, he waved good morning to the approaching man.

"I say, I don't suppose a man came by you, did he? Green coat and in a hurry?"

The man was puffing a little himself but when he stopped to reply, he looked back the way he had come. "I certainly did. He sure was in a hurry."

Albert grimaced. "I don't suppose you recognised him?"

The man's eyebrows climbed his head. "No, sorry. Did he take something from you?" He was looking for a reason why Albert might be giving chase.

"What? No, nothing like that. Are you all right? You seem rather out of breath," Albert pointed out, struggling to get his own breathing under control.

The man grinned in a self-deprecating way. "I've been walking this route every morning for six months. My doctor insists I need more exercise." He cupped his belly with a wry smile. "I can't say I enjoy it, but I have lost a few kilos."

Rex paid the man no attention, his nose aimed beyond him in the direction their quarry went. Strangely, he was getting no scent other than the one from the man his human currently spoke with. It made his ears twitch in thought.

The man aimed an index finger in his direction of travel. "Do you mind? I ought to be getting to work."

Albert thanked him for stopping and apologised for interrupting his morning walk. With the man continuing on his way, Albert stared back in the direction of the dig site, indecision bringing a deep frown.

He had every right to walk away and label the incident as 'none of his business' but certain the decision would haunt him for the rest of the day, he went back to the excavations.

Chapter 6

Albert's eyes bugged out on stalks. Was he really seeing what he thought he was seeing?

Taking care to go around the ditches, he made his way to Captain Allard, calling out to get the senior police officer's attention long before he got to him.

"What do you think you are doing?" he demanded to know.

Captain Allard's officers paused to observe the exchange. Captain Allard frowned, but didn't respond.

"I asked what you are doing?" Albert aimed an arm at the ditch that no longer contained Bjorn's body. "You haven't had the time to process the scene yet. Why are your people moving the body?"

"This is not a matter for civilians," Captain Allard chose to be dismissive. "Please be on your way, Mr Smith."

Rex continued to sniff the air, confirming what he already knew to be true. There was a body in the ground not far from where they now stood and it had been there for some time. The smell was quite unmistakable, and he could only wonder how it was that the humans didn't smell it too.

Albert was stunned. His initial impression of the captain was that of a competent man, knowledgeable and experienced. However, removing the body and letting his officers trample all over the ground around it was amateur in the extreme.

"Please tell me you already know who committed the murder then," Albert almost begged to hear they had someone in custody who chose to confess. That would make things a little better, but still failed to explain the shoddy approach to evidence gathering. Even with a confession, an airtight case was needed to ensure the guilty party couldn't wriggle free on a technicality when they later changed their minds about going to jail for their crime.

"Murder?" Captain Allard questioned, his tone scoffing. "I'm afraid not. This man was drinking last night and had a few too many. He returned to the dig site and fell over in the dark, striking his head on a rock when he plunged into one of the ditches. It is a terrible accident, but his footprints can be traced across the dirt."

"And what about the other footprints?" Albert fought to keep his temper. "Your officers have walked all over the area. If the killer left his footprints behind, they have been eradicated now. Are you completely incompetent?" He could have pointed out that the force required to crack a human skull was significantly more than a person would generate falling a few feet into a hole, drunk or otherwise. He did neither thing though, for he could see the rock on which Bjorn had supposedly struck his skull.

It was half covered in blood, the bright red faded to a dull brown. Looking around the field to confirm what he already knew to be true, Albert noted that it was the only rock in sight. The victim fell and met his end when his head collided with the only rock in the field.

No detective in the world was going to believe that story.

"*What about the body in the ground?*" asked Rex. When his human turned around to go back to the excavations, he assumed they were going to expose the second victim. That wasn't happening though, and the people were talking too fast for him to keep up.

Captain Allard wasn't used to being spoken to in such a manner and most especially wasn't going to tolerate it in front of his own officers. Storming across the dirt, he was about to give Albert a severe dressing down that might result in his arrest if he didn't learn some humility and apologise. However, Albert spoke again before he could, and it stopped him in his tracks.

"Why are you deliberately covering up this murder?"

Chapter 7

Arriving back at Le Bratzala, the three-storey guesthouse owned and run by Celeste Darroze, Albert still had the bag containing the bretzels he bought at the bakery. They were cold now and less appetising.

He fed one to Rex, who gulped it down as swiftly as the first, and threw the last one in the bin, much to his dog's disappointment.

Trying to force the unexpected events of his morning from his mind, Albert found a quiet corner of the house in which to relax and read a book. Rex settled on the carpet next to Albert's chair, stretching out and falling asleep while Albert battled to stay focused on the story.

For a moment he'd believed Captain Allard was going to arrest him. Until Albert got under his skin the man had been cool and in control, deploying his assets to get the job done. Unfortunately, the job they were tasked to do was the wrong one. They should have been collecting forensic evidence and the fact that they weren't sparked too many questions in Albert's head.

When he outright accused the police chief of covering up a murder, the man reacted with bluster and a raised voice. That was to be expected, but almost as quickly the man wrestled his ire under control, simmering down to then dismiss Albert's concerns as though they were nothing more than the amateurish questions of an uneducated layman.

They were nothing of the sort.

He told Captain Allard about the man watching through the woods and how he ran away the moment he was spotted, but even that news failed to get him to react. Bjorn was to be classified as an accidental death, a drunken misadventure and nothing more.

But what was Albert to do about it? He'd been retired for two decades, and though his mind was as sharp as ever, he had no good reason to get involved.

Except he wasn't entirely sure he could do anything else.

Closing his book, Albert pursed his lips. He was going to ask a few questions, just to satisfy his own curiosity, nothing more. If he didn't come away feeling like there was a case to investigate, he would walk away. His European trip was supposed to be a tour that took him to the birthplace of its finest culinary treats. He wanted to visit Naples for pizza, Athens for gyros, and Vienna for Wiener Schnitzel.

His first stop in Antwerp for waffles should have been a peaceful affair, yet it proved to be anything but. Again it was his old school approach to problems and life in general that caused his involvement – when he saw a problem, especially when it involved someone vulnerable, he just couldn't walk away.

Getting caught up in local events had done him no good in the past. Although, in retrospect, Albert had to admit he rather enjoyed the adventure it brought, even if it did get a little fraught at times.

He was due to meet his neighbours, Roy and Beverly, in Germany in two weeks' time and had no intention of missing their planned rendezvous. However, rising from his chair, Rex's head lifting from the carpet to see where his human was going and if he too needed to get up, Albert decided it might be fun to have something interesting to tell them.

With a click of his tongue to get Rex moving, he set off through the guesthouse in search of the landlady. He wanted to know where the Swedish dig team were staying, and in such a small village, he was willing to bet she would know.

Celeste possessed the appearance of a stereotypical grandmother. White hair set into curls clung to her head. She peered at the world through bifocal lenses and her slightly pear-shaped hips had been hidden behind an apron every time Albert had seen her thus far. She even had the contented smile of a matriarch, but Albert spotted the absence of a wedding band on her hand the moment she greeted his arrival and the house was devoid of family pictures that ought to have shown her brood of children and grandchildren.

Too polite to enquire, despite his curiosity, Albert believed the guesthouse owner to be a spinster. He found her in the kitchen where she was adding flour to a bowl.

He recognised that she was baking a cake; a form of alchemy he'd never mastered even with expert tuition.

He started by asking her what she was making.

"Oh, I have quite a bit of baking to do today, actually. I'm in a bit of a rush to tell you the truth. No time to waste."

Albert got that she was politely telling him to make it quick and go away, so he got right to the point.

"Oh, they are in Arthur's place on Rue de Paris," Celeste replied. "Are you interested in archaeology?"

Unsure how best to break the news, Albert chose to blurt it out. "No, I'm afraid one of their team was murdered last night."

Having turned to face her guest, the mixing bowl of cake batter and a spatula in her hands, Albert was perfectly placed to observe Celeste's head snap up to see if he was somehow joking. The bowl slipped between her shocked fingers, and though Albert moved fast to intercept it, the heavy bowl had a head start and gravity on its side.

It hit the tile floor with a thump, breaking, rather than smashing, the pieces held in place by the thick batter inside.

Rex's mouth dropped open. "*Yay!*" he barked, launching forward to thrust his face into the sugary mix.

Albert wasn't fast enough to stop him, the yank he gave Rex's lead doing nothing more than taking out the slack.

"*Ooh, yum,*" Rex gulped down mouthfuls of the cake batter, aware he was now in a race to consume as much as possible before the old man stopped him.

Albert yelled, "No, Rex!" He wanted to ask Celeste if she was okay and learn why her reaction to his news was so extreme. That was going to have to wait though because Rex was going to swallow a piece of broken crockery if he didn't stop the stupid dog.

With his lead now taut, Albert had to walk backward to drag Rex away.

"*Mmmf, mmmf, nooooo*!" Rex dropped his belly to the floor and dug in with his claws, trying anything to get another mouthful of the delectable cake mix.

Mercifully for Albert, there was nothing on which his dog could find purchase, so while Rex was a deadweight, the process of dragging him across the kitchen floor wasn't all that hard once he was moving.

A slug trail of cake batter followed Rex whose face was coated liberally in the gooey mess. It was in his whiskers, plastered around his muzzle, and even in his eyebrows.

"Dear Lord," muttered Albert, silently cursing in his head. Hooking Rex's lead over the door handle, he said, "Now sit there and clean yourself up, you greedy hound."

Rex did just that, using his tongue to find every last smudge.

Celeste, now that she'd been given a moment to collect herself, was crouched to deal with the broken bowl and the few dollops of cake mixture Rex wasn't fast enough to consume.

"I'm terribly sorry about that," Albert apologised. "You must let me pay for the damage."

Celeste rose to her feet, waving dismissively. "There's really no need. Besides, I was the one who dropped it."

"Yes," Albert began, "you seemed quite shocked by the news. I should have been more sensitive. I suppose you don't get many murders in these parts."

Celeste chose not to respond to what felt like a question, but said, "I just wasn't expecting it, Mr Smith. I saw the archaeologists only yesterday. They seemed to be in a fine mood. It's so shocking that something could have happened to one of them." She made a thoughtful face before asking, "Which one was … which one is no longer with us?"

"Bjorn. I'm afraid I didn't catch his last name, but he had long blonde hair." Albert motioned around his neck, indicating the length of hair as if such a gesture was needed.

Celeste put a hand to her chest, unable to hide that the news was making her feel a little faint.

"Goodness. They were all so young." As if suddenly remembering something, she looked up and into Albert's eyes. "You asked where they are staying. Why did you want to know? In fact, how is it that you know about the ... murder," she struggled to use the word, "already?"

Albert took a moment to explain that Bjorn's body was found at the dig site and how he'd heard Julienne's cry of alarm when she found him. However, he glossed over the part about why he asked where the Swedes were staying and completely left out how Captain Allard was treating the obvious murder as an accident.

He still hadn't decided what he was going to do, but sitting on his hands wasn't in Albert's nature.

Checking once again that Celeste was over her initial shock and in no danger of fainting, he withdrew, taking Rex with him. The dog needed a wash. Well, to be honest, he needed a bath; it had been weeks since Albert last forced Rex into a full body clean, but their room wasn't the place to perform such a task and he wasn't about to ask the landlady for a dozen extra towels – the minimum amount required. Rex's coat acted like a sponge and he no longer had the strength to lift him from the bath; it was just too much weight too far in front of his body. That meant Rex would leap from the tub when Albert finally decided he was clean and in so doing take a tidal wave of water with him.

A simple facewash would have to suffice. Rex had been working on the cake batter stuck to his fur for more than five minutes, but either couldn't see the furthest extremities or couldn't reach them. Either way, Albert refused to take his dog out in public with his fur stuck out at angles like some new-age canine punk.

"Come on, dog," Albert sighed at the foot of the stairs. "Let's get you clean."

Rex's ears twitched at the familiar word and his eyes doubled in size.

"*Hell, no!*" he placed his front paws against the second step and locked out his legs. "*Uh-uh. No mister. No thanks. I'll pass.*"

Realising his error, Albert let his shoulders slump. How was it that his dog could be so intuitive one moment, and eating a three-day-old kebab out of the gutter the next?

"I'm not going to put you in the bath, Rex," Albert attempted to explain.

"*Bath!*" Rex reacted to the word he feared above all others. Well, all others with the exception of castration. He knew of many, many dogs whose humans thought it a good idea to lighten their trouser area. If the old man so much as introduced the subject, Rex was going on the road by himself. Living rough had to be better than the alternative.

Now struggling to keep hold of his bucking dog, Albert tried hard to instil some calm. "No, I'm NOT putting you in the bath, Rex. I just need to get the cake out of your face."

"*Cake?*" Rex queried, his struggles subsiding so he could check the old man's plans. Was he willing to exchange a bath for cake? It was a tough choice to balance. He knew what cake was and couldn't correlate the gooey mix he'd devoured with the light, fluffy yumminess the term 'cake' represented.

Gently tugging his lead, Albert coaxed, "It won't take a minute. I just need some water to get the batter out of your fur."

Now convinced the old man was trying to trick him with false promises of cake that would magically fail to ever materialise, Rex unlocked his legs, pretending to comply. The moment his human started up the stairs again, Rex backed out of his collar and legged it.

Albert uttered a few choice words and gave chase.

Chapter 8

Lars Stromberg had his hands on his hips and his eyes closed. Things were not going to plan. No, it was distinctly worse than that. Things were about as far from plan as they could be.

To start with the map was proving to be widely inaccurate. It was a mercy no one had questioned why there were so many test trenches. All he needed was a real archaeologist to come along and they really would be in trouble.

A small snort of amusement escaped his nose. That they had not been exposed as the fakes they were was perhaps the only thing still going his way.

Ten percent. That was what they stood to gain if they found it. The estimated worth was great enough that ten percent would tide him over for the next few years. But they hadn't found it, and he wasn't sure how much longer their lie about the Stone Age settlement would stand up to scrutiny.

There were mutterings among the villagers and sideways glances to show they were discussing the Swedish archaeologists in their midst.

To his knowledge no Stone Age Settlement had ever been established near this area, but the locals appeared blithely oblivious to that inconvenient fact. So far, at least, but surely one of them had to be curious enough about local history to want to investigate for themselves.

His employer had dreamt up the lie, assuring him it always worked. The Stone Age was so long ago no one expected them to find anything exciting, thus they would pay little attention.

Lars' was just one team deployed to find that which was buried so very long ago. In spots right across the European mainland, there were others performing the exact same task. They would be doing better though, he was convinced of it. His counterparts, none of whom he had ever met or could even name, would already have called in to report their success.

If he failed to find the spot, he would not get paid and his chances of being offered a second site to excavate would be close to nil. On top of that, his failure would make it all the harder for someone else to pick up where he left off.

His eyes snapped open. Feeling sorry for himself wasn't going to get the job done.

Bjorn's death was unfortunate. It brought them attention they were trying hard to avoid, but the local head of the police appeared determined to label the death as an accident. That made no sense to Lars; his colleague's skull had been cracked on a hunk of rock that was not in the trench when they left the dig site the previous day. Yet if the police were incompetent, it played into his hands. He could ill afford an investigation that would instantly identify their university identification as fake.

Julienne was upset about Bjorn's death; she clearly liked him a little more than she ought, but she understood just as well as Lars that they couldn't make waves about it. Police incompetence was a gift at this stage.

And it wasn't as if they knew Bjorn. The four of them had only met ten days ago.

They would be extra vigilant, just in case there was something more going on than seemed apparent. Lars doubted it would be the case though. The overly pretty Bjorn attracted ladies like moths to a particularly bright light. He had undoubtedly bedded the wrong woman and found himself the victim of her husband's rage.

They needed to act the part of the recently bereaved, but would announce their intention to continue their archaeological survey in Bjorn's honour. *It's what he would have wanted.* That's what they would say.

Giving himself a mental kick in the backside, Lars picked up his coat and went to find the others.

Chapter 9

In his room, Albert employed one corner of a hand towel to carefully remove the clumps of cake batter. Rex's flight through the house resulted in two knocked over chairs, one spilled houseplant, and an elderly guest almost having a heart attack.

He couldn't open any of the doors though, so found himself cornered when Albert finally caught up.

"*Stupid humans and their stupid doors,*" Rex mumbled under his breath, expressing his feelings even though what he mostly felt was relief since Albert was showing no signs that he planned to put him in the bath.

Hearing the front door of the guesthouse open and close, Albert glanced out of the window. Celeste was hurrying down the street, a winter coat pulled tight around her shoulders.

Had she not just claimed that she had a lot of baking to do and no time to waste?

"She probably needs a new bowl," Albert told himself, but then recalled the shelf of bowls in the kitchen. There were many just like the one she dropped. "Ingredients then," he countered his own argument, but that didn't work either because he'd seen the eggs, flour, sugar, and more all lined up on the kitchen countertop.

Forcing his frown away, Albert assumed she had another errand to run or that she felt the need to spread the gossip about the murdered Swedish archaeologist. In a quiet village, he supposed it might be nice to have something juicy to share.

With Rex's fur looking clean, albeit a little damp in places, Albert knew it was time to press on with his day. His stomach had started to rumble more than half an hour ago, so he had multiple reasons for venturing out again.

He didn't know where to find Chez Anais et Marc – the place where the Swedish team of archaeologists were staying, but the village was small enough that he was happy to wander. He could always ask if it proved to be elusive. Celeste had told him what street it was on, but his memory chose to play games, hiding the name in a dark corner of his brain.

It turned out not to matter because he found the guesthouse in the very next street.

Rex couldn't work out what to do about the second body. He could smell it was there sure enough, but getting the humans to pay attention was never easy. Somehow, he was going to have to convince or trick the old man into returning to the excavations. Maybe once they were there he could hope to 'do a little digging'. Exposing the body was sure to get the message across.

Busily thinking about whether to be patient and wait for his human to take him back to the dig, or slip away so he could return to the site of his own accord, Rex jumped when a person stepped out right in front of his face.

Albert had been about to enter Chez Anais et Marc through the main entrance when it opened inward, and Julienne barrelled out. She was with Peter, the fourth member of the archaeology team.

"Oh, hello again," he offered them both a smile. Their expressions were fiercely murderous, Julienne's in particular, though Albert could see their anger wasn't aimed at him. "Is everything all right?" he enquired, doing his best to sound concerned but casual – he wasn't *really* asking questions to get to the bottom of what was going on.

Julienne's features softened, a sigh escaping her as she forced the rage from her face.

"I'm sorry about earlier," she twisted to her right to include Peter. "This is the gentleman I told you about. The one I threatened with a knife."

"That's perfectly all right, my dear. I should have done more to explain my presence."

"No, no, you were perfectly within your rights to be there. I overreacted. I hope I didn't scare you."

Albert cracked a smile. "I've been threatened with a knife before, my dear." When Julienne and Peter shot him shocked expressions, he sniggered, "I was married for many years."

It was a moment of lightness on a dark day and as he'd hoped, it gave them both a smile. It had broken the tension, and now that he had them semi-trapped outside their guesthouse, Albert threw in a question.

"Listen, I don't wish to pry, but the police don't seem to be taking your friend's death seriously. I used to be a police detective in England, and I know the difference between a person who fell and hit their head and one who was attacked with a blunt instrument."

He watched their expressions, expecting to see relief that there was someone else who believed their colleague's death was no accident. However, the glance that passed between Peter and Julienne could only be described as nervous.

It made Albert's brain itch. Lars had also behaved in an incongruous manner when he arrived at the dig site and saw his dead colleague. His concern hadn't been for Bjorn, or Julienne for that matter.

Speaking for the first time, Peter said, "Thank you. We are just on our way to the police to question their ruling."

Julienne's right eyebrow twitched in question, but she said, "Yes, that's right. We just want to make sure they have thought of everything. Bjorn was very dear to us and a valued member of our museum staff."

"Will you be returning to Sweden?" Albert enquired though he wasn't sure why it occurred to him to ask the question.

Again it was Peter who provided the answer. "No. We don't think so. Our emotions are a bit raw at the moment – I'm sure you can understand that – so we are giving ourselves a little time to absorb this shocking event. However, Bjorn really believed in what we hoped to achieve here, and I believe we will persevere in his honour."

Julienne's sad smile echoed Peter's words.

Unable to stop himself, Albert asked, "Are you not concerned that the killer is going to get away with your friend's murder?" The question was met with awkward expressions, neither Peter nor Julienne were sure how to respond, so Albert posed another, "What if the killer wasn't targeting Bjorn specifically, but your group as a whole? What if he isn't done?"

He hadn't exactly meant to scare them, but their faces showed that they were yet to consider that angle. There was no reason for Albert to think the killer was after the archaeologists. I mean, why would anyone? Nevertheless, there was something off about the way they were behaving and it was making his detective's nose twitch.

Julienne looked up at her colleague.

"I didn't ... I mean ..." she stuttered.

"Maybe we should talk to Lars," suggested Peter, already reaching for the door to go back inside. There was a tremble in his voice; nerves showing themselves again.

They collided with each other in their haste to get back inside and neither person spared Albert a parting glance.

He watched them go, curious about what he'd just seen. Captain Allard's behaviour was unexplained. The Swedish archaeology team were acting as strangely, and now that he was thinking about it, his landlady reacted in an unexpected manner too.

Just what had he stumbled across this time?

Chapter 10

Chez Anais et Marc looked as good a place to eat as any other, and the waft of garlic that exited the door when Julienne and Peter ducked back inside, lodged in Albert's nostrils where it now refused to leave.

Rex required no encouragement whatsoever, happily wagging his tail when they were led to a table.

"You ate a cake this morning," Albert pointed out, instructing Rex to lie down.

Grumpily, Rex complied. He wasn't hungry – no more than he ever was, but what did that have to do with anything? The food smells in the restaurant were enough to drive him insane, so he closed his eyes, tuned them out, and prayed his human wouldn't take too long eating his midday meal.

A little more than an hour later, Albert exited Chez Anais et Marc, his belly distinctly fuller than it had been. There had been too many wonderful options to choose from, so though he wouldn't normally eat a heavy lunch, his singular mouthful of breakfast bread convinced him to order something more substantial.

Now he regretted it.

"*Over did it, did you?*" Rex huffed. He would normally get a plate to lick or a few titbits from the side of Albert's. Today he got nothing and was a little miffed about it.

Feeling that a nap might be in order, but knowing Rex would need some exercise first, Albert aimed his feet in the direction of the village's central park. A narrow, yet constantly flowing river, ran through it, the planners having perhaps selected the area to remain free of construction quite deliberately however many centuries ago such decisions were made.

There he could let Rex off the lead and let him run while he walked off some of his overindulgent lunch. The second glass of wine had probably been unwise too, Albert mused, though when in France …

Problematically, the 'when in France' excuse could be applied to all manner of situations.

Reaching the park, he stopped Rex so he could unclip his lead.

Rex put his nose to the ground and began to sniff. There were lady dogs in the area.

Albert watched him go, questioning, not for the first time today, what he would do if his casual investigation led to something more intriguing and substantial and he found there was a need for backup. In England, he'd always known he could pick up the phone to any one of his three senior police detective children and be assured they would drop whatever they were doing to come to his rescue. Heck, they had done so multiple times even when he hadn't asked.

On the other side of the Channel it wasn't such an easy thing for them to do. The journey time was longer for a start.

During his lunch, both before it was served and while he consumed it, Albert examined the case in his head. A purely mental exercise, he attempted to assemble a working theory for why Captain Allard wanted to class the murder as an accident.

He didn't get very far. It was perplexing, and the only idea that remained, once he'd dismissed all the others as just plain silly, was that the region's senior police officer was somehow involved. Not that he was necessarily the killer, but that he knew, or at least suspected, who was. It felt like a dangerous concept and he had no intention of voicing it, yet it remained the one theory he couldn't entirely dismiss.

But why hadn't his officers said something? They couldn't all be complete newbies fresh from the academy.

"Excuse me? Hello?" called a voice from behind Albert. He spun around to see who was there, expecting to find the gentle voice belonged to a young woman. He wasn't to be disappointed, but as though the lady in question had been reading his mind about Captain Allard's officers, she was in uniform. What's more, he recognised her from the dig site.

"Hello," the young woman said again. She had blonde hair pulled upward into a short ponytail, and freckles across her nose and cheeks. They made her look younger than Albert believed she was, guessing her age to be somewhere around twenty-five. Standing five feet and five inches, she was average height for a woman, but short next to Albert. The bulky uniform hid her figure, but Albert could tell she retained the trimness of youth.

"Hello," Albert replied. "Can I help you? Is my dog supposed to be on his lead?" He looked around for any signs that might instruct patrons of the park in the correct etiquette and looked about to see if Rex might have left something offensive on the grass already.

"You are Albert Smith, no?" the officer sought to confirm, holding back from revealing her reason for stopping him until she had an answer.

Groaning a little inside, Albert suspected he knew what the young woman's question was really about. She knew who he was. She knew what he had done with Earl Bacon, and she most likely wanted a selfie so she could show her friends. He'd been silently suffering such attention for months in the UK and it was one of the primary drivers for leaving home on another adventure.

Nodding, and telling himself to be both humble and charitable, he said, "Yes, I am. Would you like a selfie?"

The woman's eyebrows performed a little dance, her features unsure what expression to choose.

"A selfie?" she questioned.

Sensing that he might have misread her intentions, Albert said, "Nevermind. How can I be of assistance?"

"The victim this morning, Bjorn Ironfoundersson, he was murdered."

Albert skewed his lips to one side. This was not what he expected.

"Go on," he encouraged.

"My boss says it was an accident. A, how do you say, open and closed case?"

"But you think otherwise?"

She pulled a face; one that conveyed how ridiculous she found the situation.

"I am the least experienced officer here, but that didn't look like an accident to me."

"What do your colleagues think?"

"They told me not to interfere. I have to be careful who I speak to, most of the police here are from the same family. Captain Allard's family. Three of my colleagues are his sons and he has two nephews and a niece on the force too."

Albert nodded along. Nepotism occurred in the UK police but not often; it had been rooted out long ago. Recommending a sibling or offspring for a role or a promotion was as likely to see them denied the chance to be considered as it was to get them the job. Out here in the sticks though …

Questions were forming a queue, but he chose one that he wanted to get out of the way.

"You know who I am? I mean, am I correct to assume you know that I have been in the papers recently, and why?"

"Yes."

"Then I have to ask why it is that you have chosen to approach me today. What is it that you want from me?"

The woman's cheeks flushed a deep scarlet; she hadn't thought this part through. She had wanted to be a cop for as long as she could remember, but now that she was out of the academy, the life she yearned for was nothing like reality. Nothing much ever happened, and now that there had been a murder, the first in as long as anyone could remember, she felt that she was witness to some kind of bizarre cover up.

The simplest and most obvious thing to do was listen to her colleagues and keep her mouth shut. The one thing she knew for certain was how little she knew about anything. Nevertheless, she saw the wound to the man's skull and the rock that had no place where it was in the field. When Albert shouted at her captain, he gave voice to all the thoughts in her head.

It had been as though he was reading her mind. At the time, she believed she recognised the old man. There was something about his giant dog that tickled her memory, so back at the station she looked up his name and that led her to seeking him out the moment her shift ended.

However, now that she was here with the perceptive old man asking her what she wanted, the truth was that she didn't exactly have an answer.

"Help me solve the case?" she replied, her voice weak and subservient as though she was checking it was an okay thing to ask.

Chapter 11

Albert twisted at the waist, looking around to spot a park bench.

"Shall we sit?" he suggested, his feet already moving. He settled at one end of the bench, angling his body at forty-five degrees so he could face her.

When she took the opposite corner, he asked, "Shall we start with your name?"

The young woman's cheeks flushed again, embarrassed to have forgotten such a simple thing.

"Margot Dubois."

Albert extended his hand. "Pleased to meet you, Margot." They shook hands, Albert noting how small and childlike hers felt in his old, calloused mitt. "Margot, I want to ask if you have really thought this through. Let's say that we uncover that Bjorn Ironfoundersson was indeed murdered. To whom will you report the crime? If your boss is guilty of incompetence, he will take a dim view to the very fact that you have doubted his ruling. He may go so far as to fire you, but at the very least, if you publicly prove him wrong, you will find yourself sidelined and marked forever more."

Margot swallowed visibly, the action confirming Albert's expectations: the potential blow back was greater than she had considered.

Pushing on, he said, "Worse yet, if there is a reason why Captain Allard chose to label the obvious murder as an accident, such as he was paid to do so, or is in some way connected to or even responsible for the murder, your prying will not result in dismissal, but will paint a fat target on your back. Are you prepared for all that?"

Albert wasn't trying to scare the poor girl. In truth he wanted to have someone in uniform on his side and questioned whether there might be others in the local police who saw things the same way as Margot. Nevertheless, he knew it would be remiss if he failed to point out the potential pitfalls.

While he waited for Margot to respond, Albert cast his eyes around the park to find Rex. His dog was apt to wander off at times.

Rex was snuffling by some holly bushes on the far side of the park. His head was down, his nose at the ground, and his brain was working overtime.

The man they found in the ditch came through the park something less than twenty-four hours earlier. Rex trusted his nose enough not to question it. He entered from the south near the stream and walked the path, but he stopped to vomit in a garbage receptacle next to a bench. The vomit was still in the bin where Rex couldn't get to it, but the man was a poor aim, and had missed in places.

Rex could smell the alcohol present and knew from his own experience with red wine that it meant the man had overindulged. With regret, Rex recalled drinking his fill of the tasty beverage when he found himself trapped in the Gastrothief's larder.

However, it wasn't so much the scent of the man that held his interest, but the scent that overlayed it. The odours were too old for Rex to be certain, but one appeared to follow the other. A second man took the same route as the first at about the same time. Both smells were faint now, carried away by time and the breeze, but sufficient lingered for Rex to be able to separate and catalogue the highs and lows of the scent profile.

What did it mean though? The first man, the drunk one, ended up dead. Rex had long since given up attempting to fathom human behaviour. It was inexplicable at the best of times, but their need to kill each other over such trivial matters was the most bizarre.

He would get into a fight over a mate for sure, but neither dog would enter the affray intending to leave the other dead. Once beaten the loser would withdraw. Why make it more complicated?

Lifting his head, Rex looked around to check where his human had gotten to. His human was apt to wander off at times. Finding the old man sitting on a bench talking with a young, female human, Rex relaxed and returned to the scents.

He thought he recognised the second scent but wasn't sure where from. That in itself was perplexing because he was very good at recalling smells. Regardless, it belonged to a man wearing Davidoff Cool Water aftershave, a generic supermarket brand deodorant, leather shoes that had not been polished in some time, and he'd eaten a considerable amount of garlic in the hours before walking the park path.

Others had walked the path since, but the strength of their scents, and the fact that they were almost all accompanied by a dog allowed him to dismiss them.

Was the scent of the second man at the ditch where they found the first man's body? Yet again Rex felt the tug to return to the scene of the crime. Only there could he make confirmation, and there was still the small matter of the second body to deal with.

Back on the other side of the park, Margot reached a decision.

"I think I am supposed to do this. If I don't, I might as well quit because it will make me a coward and a sellout. I need to know if this was murder or not, and if it is then I must know why Captain Allard wants to label it otherwise."

Albert puffed out his cheeks and nodded. It would be condescending to say that he was proud of her, but that was what it boiled down to. Moral courage is a rare thing to find; he saw it all too rarely in his career and invested much effort into instilling such a tough value into his children. They all grew to make him proud, and Margot now showed the same determination to do what was right rather than that which would prove easy.

"Okay, Margot. We must start by retracing Bjorn's steps. He was out in La Obrey drinking last night by all accounts. There will be people who saw him and saw who he was with. He may have left with a woman." Albert paused, reminding himself to keep an open mind. "Or a man," he added, uncertain of the Swede's sexual preferences. "There will be someone who was the last person to see him alive and in most cases that person turns out to be the killer."

"I'm ready."

Albert shook his head. "No, Margot, you are not. For this you will need to change your clothes."

Chapter 12

"Are they leaving?" the question hung in the air.

Across from the person who posed the question, an answer came from a voice with authority, "No, I don't believe they are. They appear to want to continue their work in their dead colleague's honour."

A timid whimper from another person drew attention their way. "Who killed him?"

"That we do not know."

"Well someone knows," snapped a new voice, that of a man in his later years. "Someone took a rock to his head. Scare them off, that was the decision, not commit murder."

The room fell silent, each person present keeping their own thoughts for a beat.

"What can we do now?" asked the timid voice. "Do we ... do we move the body?"

"The grave was never marked," replied the authoritative voice. "Unless you are able to tell me any different."

No one replied, confirming what the voice of authority believed. "Then moving the body is not an option. We have to hope their excavations fail to find it."

"Hope?" questioned the elderly voice. "That's our best strategy?"

The man who spoke with authority drew a deep, slow breath through his nose. "I am all ears if anyone has a suggestion."

No one said it, but more than one person in the room questioned if Bjorn Ironfoundersson's killer was in the room. When the notification came that an archaeological excavation was going to take place and they discovered the proposed location, their response was immediate panic. They opposed the application to conduct the dig, but even completing the paperwork they knew their reasons were weak.

It wasn't as though they could tell the truth.

So they tried to find the burial site, but in the vast field they had no clue where to look, only a rough idea. They buried the body fifty years ago and no one could remember exactly where. The landscape was mostly unchanged, but new trees had grown, so even those among them who helped to dig the grave expressed uncertainty about where to begin. They could narrow it down to a general area, but no one wanted to start digging. What were they supposed to do with the body if they found it?

Trusting the excavations would be anywhere other than the rough area they suspected, they were dismayed to see the Swedish team set up their test digs in precisely the one spot they wished them to avoid.

That led to further scheming and the idea that they might find a way to scare them off. Could they make them all ill? They were taking their meals in the village so that appeared to be one solution. Maybe it would be a short-term fix and the team would return, but they needed to try something – inaction was no longer an option.

However, when they first tried to doctor their meals, three of the plates were mixed in the kitchen, the waitresses delivering them to the wrong table. People got sick, but not the right ones.

So someone, possibly because they were bored with the group's progress, chose to take matters into their own hands. But who?

At least two of those present could be ruled out due to their age and dwindling physical ability. Bjorn Ironfoundersson was a man in his prime - strong and capable. A rock to the head might defeat even the toughest out there, but the strength to wield it was still a requirement.

That left plenty of suspects though, and the group, who were already mistrustful of each other, were growing warier still.

"There is one other element we have yet to consider," announced an as yet unheard from voice in the corner of the room. When all eyes swung his way, he continued to say, "Albert Smith."

"Albert Smith?" repeated more than one of those present.

"Yes, he's an English sleuth. You may have read about him in the paper. Or seen him on television a few months ago."

The man who spoke with authority swore. "I knew he looked familiar."

"He was at the dig site this morning when they found the body," the man who introduced Albert as a subject explained, "and is known for sticking his nose where it isn't welcome."

The room's occupants looked about at one another. It was yet another worrying element to a truth that had remained hidden for five decades. Was it really about to be exposed?

Chapter 13

Albert agreed to see Margot later and sent her away to change out of her police uniform. Her shift, due to the body they found this morning, had lasted almost fourteen hours and she was unable to hide that she was tired. The fatigue wasn't enough to put her off though, and she swore to be back in half an hour. They agreed to meet at a café overlooking Chez Anais et Marc, the guest house where the archaeologists were staying.

With no suspects to pick from, Albert wanted to watch what the Swedes were doing. There was something undeniably off about their behaviour and though Albert couldn't say that he pegged them as responsible for their colleague's death, he felt they were hiding something.

Albert ordered himself a slice of kugelhopf, a cake local to the region baked with Armagnac. To accompany it, he was served a coffee laced with more of the French brandy. He wasn't hungry, but if he was to sit in a café, he needed to act the part of the English tourist.

Rex spotted that his human wasn't eating the cake.

"*Need a hand with that?*" he gave a small whine.

"No, Rex. This would be bad for you."

Grumpily, Rex settled onto his paws and watched to see if any crumbs might fall.

So close to the start of winter, the days were short and the light began to fade not long after Albert settled into his chair. Conversely, the encroaching darkness made it easier for him to watch the guesthouse across the road.

It also meant he didn't see Captain Allard approaching the café until he was at the door. Not that Albert would have chosen to nip out the back to get away.

Switching his frame of view to watch the senior police officer when he entered the premises, Albert guessed correctly that his visit was no accident. He was there to speak with Albert and that meant someone was keeping tabs on his movements.

He hadn't seen anyone, but the old man behind the counter, who Albert took to be the owner, had seen fit to place a call not long after Albert settled into his chair, and had been watching him on and off ever since.

"Mr Smith," Captain Allard approached his table. "Do you mind if I join you?" It wasn't so much a question as an announcement of intent, and he was pulling out a chair before giving Albert a chance to respond. With a nod to the man behind the counter, he settled opposite, blocking Albert's view of the Swedes' guesthouse.

A waitress started to make a coffee, fulfilling a wordless request that showed Captain Allard was a regular visitor.

Rex rose to a sitting position, sniffing the air to remind himself of the man's scent. He smoked, but not the same kind of cigarettes he was used to in England. This was something else, something more raw.

"How can I help you?" Albert enquired, his tone polite.

Captain Allard held Albert's gaze for a few seconds, saying nothing until he said, "I rather think, Mr Smith, that it is I who can help you."

Albert leaned back into his chair. Crossing one leg over the other, he waited to hear what the police chief had to say.

The waitress brought the coffee, a medium sized cup filled with a dark black liquid. There was no milk or cream to accompany it, and no dainty biscuits on the saucer, but a single cube of dark brown sugar.

When she withdrew, Captain Allard turned the cup until the handle was positioned the way he wanted it, then returned to silently observing Albert. By then a minute had passed with neither man feeling a need to speak.

"This morning you found yourself in the wrong place at the wrong time, Mr Smith."

"Did I?" Albert challenged.

"Yes, Mr Smith, you did. Trust me, I have lived in La Obrey my entire life and I know how things work around here. You believe you saw something that you did not and because of who you are, you feel a natural inclination to assume there is something going on when there is not. That is why you insisted Bjorn Ironfoundersson had been murdered when nothing could be further from the truth."

Albert kept all emotion from his face when he replied. "So you are content the wound we all saw was the result of an accident."

Captain Allard gave an almost insignificant nod of his head. "Yes, Mr Smith, I am. And so should you be. La Obrey is a quiet peaceful town where nothing much ever happens. To my knowledge there has never been a murder recorded here and I can trace my family's heritage back through three generations of police work. My father was the captain before me."

"So the nepotism didn't start with you, but you have continued it? I am led to believe the majority of the officers under your command are directly related to you?"

"That is correct, Mr Smith, but hardly relevant. You seek to distract me so I shall get straight to the point."

"Please do."

"You came to this village as a tourist did you not?"

"I came to sample the local cuisine, yes."

"Then do so and be on your way, Mr Smith. There is nothing here but trouble for you if you choose to linger."

Albert's eyebrows hiked up his forehead. He'd been threatened before, but rarely by members of the law enforcement community. That Captain Allard would do so within earshot of the café owner spoke volumes about his standing and influence. He was among his own people; a respected and possibly even admired member of the village. As the police captain he could get away with a lot, but the question smashing its way to the front of the queue was whether he could get away with murder.

Reaching for his coffee, Albert watched his hand to see if it would tremble. His adrenaline had spiked, as anyone's might when given such a thinly veiled warning. His hand held steady, his worry he might rattle the cup against the saucer for naught, and he smiled at his table companion when he lifted the beverage to his lips.

"Thank you, Captain Allard, for speaking so plainly. I appreciate the advice." Albert already knew the most sensible thing for him to do was to get out of Dodge, so to speak, but he had a very old school way of looking at the world. If he didn't stick around to get to the bottom of the mystery, then who would? And how could he show such poor moral courage so soon after witnessing Margot Dubois' steel backbone?

No, he was going to play along, at least for now, but if he needed a clearer indication that Captain Allard was criminal rather than incompetent, then he had it. The local police chief wanted Albert to quietly go away and the silent subtext of his threat hung heavy in the air: or else.

Chapter 14

Captain Allard picked up his coffee cup with his right hand and scooped the sugar cube with his left, popping it between his lips. Albert watched when he let the sugar cube drop into his mouth and chased it with the still steaming black coffee.

He'd never seen anyone take their hot beverage like that before.

Gripping the arms of his chair, Captain Allard made ready to stand, but before rising said, "I knew you would be willing to see sense, Mr Smith." He aimed a nod at the café owner and left without another word, his drink either on the house or soon to find its way onto Albert's bill.

Drawing a long, slow deliberate breath, Albert reached out with his left hand to scratch Rex's ears and skull.

"I believe, old boy, that we might very well be in over our heads."

Rex heard the comment but couldn't comprehend its meaning. There was nothing new in this; humans talked gibberish half the time. He recognised the visitor who came to the table as one of the men who was at the dig site earlier, and knew a police uniform when he saw one. However, the conversation that passed between his human and the other man was not one he'd been able to keep up with.

Albert hadn't been able to see Chez Anais et Marc for the last five minutes, and sod's law dictated that the Swedes would have exited the building in that time.

Less than thirty seconds after Captain Allard left the café, Margot appeared at the door. Her eyes were aimed in the direction her boss had gone, tracking his departure to make sure he wasn't about to come back.

She fumbled for the door handle, only looking where she was going as she pushed her way inside.

Albert flared his eyes when she looked his way and mouthed, "Not here," hoping she would be wise enough to understand.

Margot looked away instantly, smiling at the man behind the counter.

"Hugo," she greeted him. "Can I get four slices of mille feuille to go, please? I'm having friends over."

Pleased that she was bright enough to devise a reason for her visit on the spot, Albert tucked into his own cake. He still wasn't hungry after his big lunch, but the plan to watch the guesthouse opposite was now a bust. Captain Allard's threat changed things. If Margot was seen with him, she might become a target too, and he suspected the café owner would report what he saw if Margot joined Albert at his table.

She paid for her cakes, accepted a small, white cardboard box from the waitress, and left the café.

Albert raised his hand to get his bill and was reaching for his wallet when his phone rang.

Retrieving it from an inner jacket pocket, he checked the screen to find it displayed the name of his youngest son.

"Randall, my boy. To what do I owe the pleasure of this call?" His mood, which had been dark all day and getting darker, lifted instantly. He had three great kids and though they worried about him far more than they needed to, he wasn't about to complain.

"I'm just checking in, Dad. Making sure you are doing okay."

"I'm just fine, son. Rex and I have been enjoying the clean air and wonderful views. The food is good too. You should visit yourself when you have some vacation days."

"Where are you again, Dad? I forget."

Albert rolled his eyes. "I'm in France."

"Yes, Dad, I meant more specifically where in France?"

"A little village called La Obrey. It's about halfway between Strasbourg and Colmar but off the beaten track."

"I'm sure it's lovely. Soooo, not getting into any trouble then?"

And there it was, the real reason for his call. Most likely Randall had drawn the short straw and it was his turn to check in on dad. Next it would be Selina or Gary who made the call. Before he left, his kids all expressed their desire that he not take another trip. Albert couldn't exactly blame them after the last one went so spectacularly sideways, but there was no good reason to believe he would encounter mayhem, murder, and mystery a second time.

No good reason, but it appeared to be happening anyway.

"Well," Albert scratched his head. He didn't want to lie to his son, but didn't want to cause him to worry unnecessarily.

"Yes, Dad," Randall sighed. "What have you gotten yourself mixed up in this time?"

"Well," Albert was frowning and trying not to sound grumpy when he said, "there was a murder here yesterday. A Swedish archaeologist was bludgeoned with a rock and left in one of his own excavation holes. The local police chief has labelled it as an accident when it clearly isn't, and the team of archaeologists are acting just as weirdly."

Randall sighed again. "Okay, Dad, but what does any of that have to do with you? There's no reason for you to get involved."

"Who said I was?"

"Oh, come on, Dad. I know you well enough to be certain you are already investigating. What are you up to right now? Staking out the Swedes? Helping some junior cop to solve the case?"

Albert's frown deepened. Was he really that predictable?

"Randall, I don't feel your tone is called for. I didn't need your help last time, and I don't need it now either."

"I'm sorry, Dad. You're right. I apologise. But you did get into quite a bit of bother last time. We are all just hoping we can avoid the same kind of trouble now that you're even farther away."

Albert forced his rising ire to dissipate. His kids were looking out for him, and Randall was generously not pointing out how much grief the previous adventure caused his children. They were all suspended from work and could have lost their jobs had he not finally caught the man behind the crime spree he chose to investigate.

"If you must know, son, I am poking my nose in," Albert relented. "Someone has to."

"But that someone doesn't have to be you."

"But I'm here, Randall. If I don't do this, no one else will."

Randall had no response to give other than to beg his father to be careful.

Slipping his phone back into his jacket pocket when the call was done, Albert thanked the waitress when she brought his change and cleared the table. With a stiff, emotionless nod to the owner, who continued to watch from his position behind the counter, Albert left the café.

It was getting dark out, the sun dipping behind the mountains even though it wasn't yet four o'clock.

"Albert."

The voice came from his left, Margot stepping out of the shadows when he turned to see who was there.

"Margot. Good, you waited for me. Sorry about the café ..."

Margot interrupted, "Hugo called Captain Allard, didn't he?"

"I believe so, yes. He came to warn me to keep my nose out of things. That might be the safest thing for you to do, you know."

Margot made a face that suggested she'd been considering the same thing. However, before she could express her thoughts on the matter, the front door of Chez Anais et Marc opened and the three remaining Swedish archaeologists stepped out. They were dressed for the cold, rugged outdoor boots on their feet and hats on their heads to keep their ears warm. It was too early for them to be heading out for dinner, but Albert was willing to bet they had something else in mind.

Chapter 15

In the dwindling light, Albert, Rex, and Margot trailed after the Swedes. Albert had already walked plenty for one day, but kept his mouth shut and did his best to keep pace with his young companion on the uphill slog through the village.

Once it was clear the Swedes were heading for the dig site, Albert slowed his pace. His knees were protesting, but he said, "We should let them get farther ahead of us. Once we leave the houses, we run the risk of them seeing us behind them. If we drop back, we can let them start doing whatever it is they are planning to do and catch them at it."

Margot agreed, but asked, "What can they do at the dig site in the dark? Why would they even want to go back there? Their colleague's blood still stains the dirt."

"But did you notice how unbothered they were by his demise? I saw Julienne this morning and she looked shocked, but that was because she'd just found the body. I've seen enough recently bereaved people to be certain all three of them ought to be more contemplative."

Margot was yet to have to deliver her first notice of death and had never until today seen a dead body unless one counted her grandmother in an open casket five years ago.

Rex was happy to be out for another walk, it was much more fun than sitting in their room or even going out to a café or bar since his human was being so stingy with the titbits today. They were following people with scents he recognised. All three were humans he'd smelled today at the dig site. He didn't know why they were following them now, but unless he was very much mistaken, they were heading back to where they found the body this morning. That meant he could finally show the old man the location of the second body.

The breeze shifted direction, the cool air swirling in from behind them. They were paused at the edge of the village, watching the now distant figures take the track around the trees.

Satisfied they could no longer be seen, Albert and Margot set off, but Rex didn't move.

"Come on, boy," Albert gave his lead a gentle tug. "Let's get going."

Rex lifted his nose a little and squinted back the way they had come. The breeze had dropped once more, denying him the chance to confirm the smell he caught a brief whiff of. Was it the same one that overlapped the victim in the park?

He could neither see nor smell the person now, but his senses screamed that there was someone behind them.

His hackles lifted, and a low growl emanated from deep inside Rex's chest.

Dropping to one knee to get his head alongside Rex's, Albert looked where his dog's eyes were aimed.

"What is it, boy?"

"What's happening?" asked Margot.

Albert couldn't see anyone in the dark street, but he'd learned to trust Rex. Dogs are known for their loyalty and German Shepherds are a preferred breed for law enforcement agencies because of their intelligence, but Rex was something else. It had taken Albert a while to realise it, but his dog wasn't like other animals. There was just no way to explain some of the things he did. He seemed to know what to do and where to go and on more than one occasion, Albert wondered if Rex was trying to tell him something. Not 'Can I have a biscuit' or 'I need to go for a walk' but more along the lines of 'Look over here, I have found a clue'.

To answer Margot, Albert said, "I'm not sure."

Rex continued to stare, but when the breeze swirled again and the scent he expected it to carry wasn't there, he let his hackles drop. He hadn't imagined it, but Rex accepted that he might be wrong. Licking his chops, he turned to face the way the humans wanted to go and with one last look over his shoulder, started walking.

"I guess it was nothing," Albert remarked.

The Swedes were nowhere in sight having made their way through the trees, but moments after leaving the protection of the houses, Albert and Margot spotted beams of torchlight coming from the direction of the dig site.

The archaeologists were back there and it looked as though they were working.

Keen to see what they were really up to, Albert and Margot didn't take the path around the woods, but made their way through them instead. Underfoot the terrain was treacherous with old brambles, fallen dead wood, and rabbit holes to snag and trip the unwary, yet they made it through without injury.

Rex pulled at his lead. "*The second body is over there somewhere. I can find it easily enough if you let me go.*"

Albert held him back, paying Rex no attention as he gawped at the archaeology team with bewildered eyes.

"Those are metal detectors," Margot whispered, close enough to Albert that he could smell her perfume and feel the warmth coming off her skin. "And they are nowhere near the trenches they dug."

Albert was used to having more questions than answers, but the latest development made no sense at all. He knew very little about how to conduct an archaeological dig, and what little he did know came from watching TV shows. However, the incongruity Margot pointed out was massive. The purpose of digging into the ground was to find that which had been left behind by settlers many centuries ago. They would want to find earthworks that showed their ancient dwellings and hope to find evidence of the food they ate, how they managed their latrines, and hopefully discover crude pots, tools, and other implements that would shed light on how the Stone Age people here might have lived.

None of that could be achieved with a metal detector.

The scene before them was almost completely silent as though someone had turned the volume down. The three archaeologists were moving across the field, waving their detectors back and forth as they searched. Albert only needed to watch for a minute to realise they were each searching a grid. They walked in straight lines, turning left or right every twenty or so yards as though mowing a lawn to create a striped pattern.

Breaking the silence abruptly, an electronic whine pierced the air and Julienne lifted her arm. The noise, which sounded quite insistent, was enough to get all three excited. Peter and Lars placed their detectors on the ground where they stood, marking their positions before hurrying over to check Julienne's discovery.

They were jabbering in Swedish, but even if Albert spoke the language, they were too far away to hear what was being said.

Their attention was wholly directed at the dirt by their feet where Julienne now dug with a trowel, throwing clumps of dirt to one side as she excavated a hole.

Bored with his feeling of confusion, Albert started toward them. Their behaviour had been odd and unexplained since he met them, but even though he didn't suspect them of Bjorn's murder they were undeniably up to something. Albert believed that whatever it was had very possibly resulted in their colleague's death.

Finding out what they were up to would at the very least solve one element of the mystery and might tell him why their friend was dead.

"Albert!" hissed Margot, hurrying to catch up. "What are you doing?"

Keeping his voice quiet – he intended to sneak up on the Swedes – Albert whispered back, "I'm going to ask them what they are doing. Whatever is going on in La Obrey, whatever got their friend killed and now has your boss issuing threats and trying to cover things up, it has something to do with whatever this bunch are doing. They probably won't want to tell me the truth, but catching them in the act will make it very hard for them to lie."

Rex thought they were going to the ditches, so when they bypassed them and he still wasn't able to show his human the site of the second body, he dug his paws into the soft earth.

Albert's arm yanked around when Rex suddenly stopped.

Rex was trying to go in a different direction, and since Albert's choices were to drag him, shout at him, or just let him go, he picked the one that meant he could continue to sneak up on the Swedish archaeologists.

Released from his lead, Rex bounded across the field, leaving the humans to do whatever it was they had in mind. Nearing the ditches, each of which was about four feet deep, Rex slowed. He needed to use his nose to find the exact spot, a task that was easier than expected.

The smell coming from the body wasn't one a human would notice, yet to Rex's canine nose it was not only unmistakable, it was powerful too. The odour was a combination of the rotting flesh, the bacteria feeding on it, escaping gases, the clothing the victim still wore, and a hundred more odours that Rex knew to associate with the location of a body.

It wasn't exposed, but lay just beneath the surface at the bottom of a trench running perpendicular to the wood line.

Across the field, Albert and Margot were approaching the Swedes. Lars and Peter were bent at the waist watching Julienne on the ground. She had dug down into the soil and was holding each trowelful over her detector.

It chose to whine, the sound followed by groans when Julienne held up something small and thin.

"Just an old nail," she reported, her voice dripping with disappointment.

Pawing the ground to shift some more of the dirt, Rex dug gently. He possessed no concept of forensic evidence, so the care he took was nothing to do with protecting the body and what might be found with it, but a wish to be able to show his human what he had found without needing to dig the whole thing up.

Exposing a foot, Rex lifted his head and barked.

The sound came from directly behind Albert and Margot, so they were framed in three beams of light when the archaeologists all snapped their heads around.

Startled, Albert nevertheless said, "Good evening. Spot of late night archaeology, is it?"

Not to be left out, Margot spat, "Why don't you tell us what you are really doing in La Obrey?"

Rex could see the humans, all five of them having a nice conversation fifty yards away across the field. Couldn't they hear him barking?

"*Oi!*" he made his bark even louder. "*Are you lot deaf? I have a dead body over here, so even if you are all too noseless to smell it, you should at least come to take a look.*"

Albert was quite curious to learn what his dog was barking about, but the three very guilty looking Swedish archaeologists were about as on the spot as a person can get and that demanded his undivided attention.

"What we are really doing?" repeated Lars, the group's leader and self-appointed spokesperson. He managed to sound haughty, but the delay between being asked and finding an answer gave away his lies before he had a chance to say them. "We are continuing our fallen comrade's fine work. That is what we are doing."

"With metal detectors?" Albert scoffed. "In a completely different section of the field to that in which you dug your trenches?"

Sneering, Lars replied, "Do you know much about archaeology, Sir?"

"Enough be feel certain only an idiot would look for a Stone Age settlement with an implement designed to find metal."

Lars' mouth opened to deliver a response, but found itself stuck in that position. His brain worked feverishly, and had it not been so cool out, he might have started to sweat from the effort.

Albert had him and neither Julienne nor Peter had anything to say that might clarify their need to go metal detecting in the dark.

"*Here,*" Rex quite literally spat, emptying his mouth in the space between the humans. "*Would you like to pay attention now?*"

Three feet above his head, the humans were all locked in a staring contest much akin to a Mexican standoff. Someone was going to have to speak, and no one wanted to be the one to do it. For Albert, he knew he possessed the upper hand. With his last remark the ball landed firmly in the Swedish court, so all he had to do was wait. The longer it took Lars to answer, the weaker his response would sound.

Julienne, her belly gripped with panic, for all their lies were being exposed, glanced down at the dog. Anything was better than meeting the old man's accusing gaze.

Except it wasn't.

Her squeal of horror broke the standoff like a hammer through a sheet of glass. Where silence broken only by the sound of the breeze existed one moment, the next it was filled with the startled, choking gasp of a person who had just seen something particularly frightening.

Having jumped half out of her skin, Margot followed Julienne's wide eyes to the ground beneath Rex's face.

Had he been aware that to do so would be funny, Rex might have said, "*Ta-dah!*" and taken a bow. Unfortunately, being a dog, comic relief wasn't really his thing.

"My God," stammered Margot. "That's a foot."

Chapter 16

J ulienne promptly about-faced and threw up.

Rex wagged his tail, proud to finally be able to display his discovery.

"*See? I told you there was a second body.*"

Margot had dropped into a crouch and using a torch taken from a coat pocket, was examining the foot.

"*There was a shoe as well,*" Rex barked, his paws dancing about in excitement. "*But I dropped it on the way over.*"

Albert bent at the waist to get his face and eyes closer to the ground. The foot was snapped off at the ankle joint, the flesh separating easily because it largely wasn't there. The foot itself then was held in place mostly by a sock, though that had rotted too, and the bones of the big toe poked through a hole, strips of dead flesh hanging from it.

Looking up at Rex, who wagged his tail even harder, Albert asked, "Where did you find it, boy?"

Rex felt like dancing a little jig. Humans were oh so fancy with their stupid apposable thumbs. Opening doors and driving cars like they were the most evolved creatures on the planet. But give him a nose that worked any day.

"*Come on! It's over here!*" he barked, the sound of it shockingly loud in the quiet field. Prancing back toward the trees, he led his human.

Margot aimed a fierce glare at Peter and Lars. Julienne was still bent over and facing the other way.

"Don't go anywhere," she warned. "There will be questions for you to answer." Upon seeing the foot - the second victim in the same field on the same day - her immediate thoughts were that the Swedish archaeologists were some kind of macabre murder club. Before she could react to that by drawing her sidearm, the logical part of her brain caught up. The foot was not a fresh kill. In fact, from the little she knew about decay from a single lecture at the academy, it had been in the ground for years.

That meant the Swedes had nothing to do with it, but they were far from off the hook. Albert was right, they were up to something. Quizzing them would have to wait though. Jogging to catch up with Albert, she watched his dog bounding and stopping, bounding and stopping, turning each time he stopped to make sure the humans were following.

"*It's over here!*" he barked, his excitement bubbling over.

Halfway to the trenches, Albert spotted a shoe. It was covered in dirt and falling apart, the sole detached from the upper around the toes and along one side. Fishing out his phone, he placed one hand against the dirt and crouched to examine his find.

The shoe was a leather loafer and might once have been brown. The colour was lost to time now, but Albert didn't think it had been black. The sole had a wear hole beneath the ball of the foot and the heel was worn down on one side. It was the well-worn shoe of a man of moderate means. Albert wondered if he might have used cardboard or something under his sock to make them more comfortable.

Rex arrived at the trench, but turned to find Albert and Margot bent over the shoe. He ran back to their position.

"*It was on the foot. I wanted to bring it to you, but when I tried to take it off the foot came with it.*"

"We're going to find a body over there, aren't we?" Margot murmured.

Albert's attention was on the shoe, and he was only half listening when he said, "That would be my guess."

Margot knew it was her job to confirm it, and her job to call it in if there was. Heck, even if there wasn't a body where the dog so keenly wanted to take them, she was going to have to call in the foot. Her attempt to work surreptitiously with the old, English sleuth had lasted less than an hour. There would be no way to hide that she was investigating Bjorn Ironfoundersson's murder. What other possible explanation could she give her boss for being back at the dig site after dark?

Following Rex, she assumed Albert would follow and set off to see what there was to see.

Albert didn't follow. His eyes were still locked on the shoe. Or rather, something protruding from it. Lodged between the upper and the sole at a point where the two were yet to separate, a piece of something colourful protruded.

He knew he ought not to touch the shoe at all. It was evidence. For that matter, the thing protruding from the leather was also evidence, but it had just been in his dog's mouth and was no longer in the position it had once been. Coupled with that his concern that Captain Allard might elect to call this a terrible accident too – 'Oh, look, the poor chap buried himself' – Albert threw caution to the wind and did what he wanted.

With a handkerchief to avoid leaving his fingerprints in the mud on the shoe, and to keep the mud from his fingers, Albert gripped the thing that was wedged in the gap between sole and upper. It came free with a little wiggling.

He felt fairly certain he knew what it was though whether that would help him or not he couldn't guess, so he wrapped his handkerchief around it and tucked the lot into his trouser pocket.

Margot was already at the trench where she had climbed down inside so only her shoulders and head were showing.

She looked up when Albert arrived, shining her torch at the exposed leg. There were claw marks raked through the damp earth, showing where Rex had performed his canine exhumation.

"Any idea who that could be?" Albert asked, holding out no hope Margot would be able to supply an answer.

"None at all," she raised her right hand for Albert to help her out of the hole. "But whoever that is, they have been in there a long time."

Rex was still prancing, his tongue hanging out and his tail wagging.

"*Are we going to stick around to solve the case,*" he asked. "*That would be fun, don't you think?*" During their previous travels, they had come across mysteries to solve almost everywhere they went. There had been people to chase, scents to track, and he got to do it all with his favourite human.

With no idea what the noises Rex made were supposed to mean, Albert ruffled the fur around his neck. "Well done, Rex. Good work."

Rex wagged his tail enthusiastically, then nudged Albert's right coat pocket, the one where he kept the gravy bones.

Chuckling, Albert took one out and handed it over, warning Rex, as he so often needed to, that the pink things were fingers. Otherwise, he stood a distinct chance of getting bitten in the process.

"I need to call this in," Margot announced, taking out her phone. She walked a few paces away, switching to French when someone answered her call.

Albert stared down into the trench. The leg was hidden in shadow, but wouldn't be for long. A team would come to exhume it from the dirt, taking their time to be sure they found all there was to find.

Would they be able to identify the victim? Would someone know who it was from his clothing? Any forensic scientist would be able to determine how long the victim had been in the ground, but whether that information would prove useful Albert could not guess.

His eyes locked on the trench, Albert's next question was the scariest: What if the victim is not alone?

Chapter 17

The police were swift to arrive, two of Margot's colleagues parking at the edge of the field behind the archaeologists' van just as they had that morning.

Margot waved her torch in the air to attract them.

Albert was getting cold and worried Rex might be too. His dog always seemed so resilient, and the temperature was above freezing, but Rex's dinner time had come and gone, and he was going to have to take him back to their accommodation soon.

Despite all that, he couldn't leave yet.

Margot showed her colleagues the trench and the body. One radioed their base, at least Albert guessed that was what he did. It was a body in a shallow grave and could not be ignored. The likelihood that the Swedish archaeologists inadvertently exposed the body and that the man in the ground was a murder victim were high.

High enough that Albert could see no other likely outcome. There were questions about the victim, but Albert's mind was more attuned to what might have happened to Bjorn Ironfoundersson. The Swedes dug a series of trenches, one exposed a murder victim, not that they noticed, but soon thereafter one of their team was killed.

In his time as a police detective Albert swore by several key principles. One of which was 'there are no coincidences in police work'. Sticking to that policy, the two murders had to be related. Someone knew the body was in the ground where the Swedes were digging and in trying to protect their secret they killed one of the archaeologists.

Leaving the police to deal with the body, Albert made his way back across the field to the team of Swedes. They were in their van, all three squeezed into the front seats where they were keeping warm with the engine running.

They saw him coming, their lips moving to show they were discussing their story and getting it straight. Albert no longer cared to hear their lies though, however well thought out they might be. The situation had moved on and though their actions were suspicious, he now had a plausible reason for their colleague's death, and they were not in the frame for it.

Lars wound down his window as Albert approached, so he went to the other side where Peter sat in the driver's seat.

He could tell they were going to start explaining their metal detection the first chance they got, so he disarmed them by speaking first.

"You uncovered a body."

Peter's worried face swung around to check with Lars who spluttered, "We did what?"

"What was Bjorn doing here last night?" Changing subject without warning was an old tactic Albert employed all the time as a detective. It kept the interviewee's wheels spinning and stopped them from being able to anticipate the next question.

This time it was Julienne who answered. "It was his turn to mind the gear and watch the site."

"His turn?"

"That's right," Lars confirmed. "We have a lot of expensive equipment here and our application to excavate the site was strenuously opposed to the point that we worried the locals might come and fill it in at night."

Albert filed the information away while nodding that they were right to worry. Someone opposed the dig and that someone must have known about the body.

"What reason did they give for opposing the dig?"

"It was because they wanted to preserve the beauty of the area," supplied Peter, looking relieved to know an answer for once.

Headlights swung into view, more police arriving Albert saw a few moments later when the moonlight caught the light bar on their roof. He was relieved to not find Captain Allard exiting the vehicle but doubted it would be long before the local chief would make his appearance.

He would have finished for the day by the time the call came in, and was likely at home having dinner with his wife, if he had one. Regardless, the news of a body would demand his attendance.

Rex sniffed around the van, sampling the smells. This was nothing more than habit on his part. His paws were wet and getting cold. It was all good fun being outside, but his stomach had been rumbling for hours, the cake batter second breakfast long forgotten now.

The scents of the people in the van were to be found near the body, but not on it, so Rex wasn't associating them with the crime. The body itself hadn't smelled of much, which is to say that the background human odours associated with the products they used and the food they ate were long gone.

He understood that there were two bodies in the same location, but could not connect them - even he could calculate the one he found in the dirt had been there a long time.

More headlights came into view, drawing Rex's attention in case they were bringing food.

Albert decided it was time to get Rex back onto his lead. He'd let him roam where he pleased thus far, confident he wouldn't stray, but the police wouldn't want a dog anywhere near the site of the body, even if he was the one who found it.

"Come along, Rex," Albert coached, stroking the fur around his shoulders and patting his flank.

The light came on inside the latest car to arrive, illuminating the people inside as they opened their doors. In the passenger seat, Captain Allard aimed disapproving eyes at Albert.

Steeling himself, Albert pushed away from the van, walking its length to stand at the edge of the field where the police chief was going to have to speak to him. He wanted to see the captain's face, to be able to judge his state of mind. Did he know about the second body? Was that why he was so willing to label Bjorn's murder as an accident? Or was it as he first suspected and Captain Allard knew the killer and was covering up the crime to protect someone?

Chapter 18

Captain Allard scowled at Albert, his face filled with something close to hatred. Albert wanted to ask him some questions. Rather pointed ones such as, 'Did you cover up Bjorn's death because you wanted to avoid an investigation that might uncover the second body?' and 'Do you know who killed Bjorn Ironfoundersson?'

However, the captain said something to the police officer who accompanied him – one of his sons given the facial similarities – and made his way across the field. The captain's son, a man in his early to mid-thirties, aimed his feet at Albert.

Albert could have shouted his questions, but he wanted to see Captain Allard's reaction and he was already twenty yards away, too far to make out his features.

He made to follow him, just to confirm what Allard's son was going to do.

"Thank you, Sir," the police officer put out his arm to halt Albert. "This is now a police matter. We know where you are staying and will come by to collect a statement later this evening or in the morning. Please do not check out or leave La Obrey until we have."

Albert met the man's eyes, holding them with his own while contemplating what to say. He could just do as instructed; they wanted him off the site so that was going to happen no matter how he protested, but his ire was up, so he tilted his head as he inspected the man before him.

"How deeply involved is your father?" It was a loaded question. He had to know there was something going on, but Albert got no sense from his wordless response that he knew what it was.

Grabbing Albert's left arm around the bicep, he tried to steer him on his way.

The growl from Rex was immediate.

"No, Rex," Albert commanded, pulling on the lead to make sure he wouldn't lunge. Looking down at the offending hand and back up at the police officer, Albert said, "I can make my own way, thank you."

The hand withdrew, but the officer held his ground, unwilling to be intimidated by an old man with a big dog. His father said the English tourist was a problem to be handled carefully, a busybody who would cause trouble and stir up drama if he was permitted to do so. That he had been present at the discovery of two bodies in the same day was enough to reinforce that concept.

He watched the old man walk away, waiting until he was out of sight behind the trees before he set off across the field to join his father. The crime scene van was on its way and there was work to do.

Albert didn't look back, but he did check out the view across the field. The moon wasn't bright enough to illuminate the ground, and the torches being flashed around made it even harder to pick out the figures gathered around the ditches.

Captain Allard's voice carried in the still, dark air, harsh tones in French which Albert didn't need to translate to know they had to be aimed at Margot. It was unfortunate that her decision to look for the truth backfired so fast, but she could feel some sense of vindication - the second body justified her quest for a different verdict regarding Bjorn's death.

That wouldn't help her yet, not unless they could prove her boss was involved somehow, so Albert hoped she was wise enough to be apologetic and meek for the time being. Any other course of action might see her fired or paint an even larger target on her back.

The downhill trek back to town was easier than the uphill slog to the field and Albert hoped it was the last time he would have to do it. In many ways he wished he hadn't taken Celeste's advice and chosen instead to remain in the village that morning. He would be oblivious to the two bodies and that would have saved him a lot of grief.

Rex plodded along at the old man's side. They were heading back to their guesthouse and that suited him just fine. His belly was empty – never a good thing for a dog – but his dinner awaited.

All in all it had been a good day. He didn't get to chase anyone and apart from the dropped bowl of cake batter, he hadn't had much to eat beyond the kibble his human served for breakfast, but life was pretty good all the same.

It wasn't in his nature to think about what the next day would bring; canine brains don't work that way. He was happy now and that was all that mattered. However, his nose, which randomly sampled the air passing it even when he wasn't paying any attention, delivered a message that interrupted his thoughts: the scent from the park was back.

Albert's nose threatened to drip. The cool air was getting to it, so he pulled out his handkerchief with a shake to loosen the scrunched-up material. With a gasp, he saw the thing he took from the shoe shoot from the folds of his once pristine white handkerchief. It tumbled through the air and into the street.

Had it not done so, the blunt instrument swung from the garden Albert and Rex were passing might have killed him. As it was, Albert's sudden change in direction to retrieve that which he had just dropped moved him just enough that the blow struck his skull and then left shoulder at a glancing angle.

Albert cried out in pain and surprise, falling away and down which took him farther out of reach.

Rex caught the man's scent only a moment earlier – too recently to have figured out where it was coming from, but now he knew because he could see him.

Three feet above them and leaning over a low fence atop a short wall to swing a golf club at Albert's head, the man now found himself silhouetted beneath a blanket of stars.

Albert could see stars too, though his were dancing across his vision as the pavement came up to meet him. Aware enough to put out his hands, he prevented his face from impacting the rough surface, and in so doing released Rex's lead.

Suddenly free, Rex's paws twitched. The man was no longer leaning over the fence and could be heard crashing through the garden. He wanted to give chase, but his human was on the ground and clearly hurt.

"*Hey*," Rex nuzzled Albert's face. "*Are you okay?*"

Albert's head felt like it was splitting in two, but he knew his injury wasn't life threatening. He also knew his attacker was getting away, so rolling limply onto his side, he used his uppermost arm to point at the garden fence.

"Rex, sic 'im!"

It was all Albert felt he could manage to say without his skull exploding, but those three words were all his dog needed to hear. If there was a better command to be given (unless it was 'eat until you are full') Rex didn't know what it could be.

With a lunge driven by powerful back legs, he took off. The garden fence was low enough that he could get over it with a run up, so that was what he did, crossing the road to give himself enough speed. A yard from the wall he converted his straight-line trajectory from horizontal to vertical. His front paws cleared the wall, landing on the fence above it as he sailed upward. His back paws scrambled for purchase on the rough brickwork, sending him to the top of the fence where he hooked his front paws, changed direction again, and sailed over it into clear air on the other side.

The man was gone, but Rex needed neither eyes nor ears to find his quarry. Now on his trail, Rex could be utterly certain the man he pursued was the same one whose scent he found at the park. There it overlapped with the body they found in the ditch this morning and Rex knew to be suspicious.

Sprinting across the garden, he followed the man over another fence, this one low enough to leap in a single bound. The man smelled of shoe polish and soap, of deodorant, sweat, and pork fat which was present at a strength Rex knew it had to have dripped onto the man's clothing.

He jumped the next fence, running through the gardens behind a row of houses. Sailing over the next fence, he spotted the man. He was two gardens ahead, a lead that would last him all of a few seconds. It was one of the best things about chasing humans, they were so slow that a dog could take their time and enjoy the chase.

Getting to play a quick game of 'chase and bite' was the perfect way to end his day, but while he felt an urge to prance like Pepé Le Pew, he resisted, put his head down and surged onward, going faster to be sure he wouldn't be denied his prize.

Leaping the next three-foot high fence, Rex saw that the distance between them had halved again. Five more seconds was all he needed to close the gap, but looking beyond the man as he came back to earth and lost sight of him once more, Rex spotted a taller fence ahead. The man was going to have to climb it to get away and that would stall his forward progress more than he could afford.

Smiling inside, Rex bounded three strides to take him across the garden and leapt once more.

The man was at the high fence, his hands gripping the top. He kicked up, using his arm strength to get to waist height. All he had to do now was roll over the fence and drop down on the other side.

Rex didn't give him the chance.

Racing forward Rex could see a choice. He could go up the fence and over it, likely landing on the other side at the same time as his human's attacker, or he could bite the backside pointed his way, sink his teeth in and yank him back down to earth before he could make it safely over the top.

The latter held greater appeal.

With a bark of triumph, Rex hit the bottom of the fence and jumped, his back legs propelling him upwards like an alligator leaping to get a roast chicken at a zoo. Mouth open, jowls pulled back, he sank his teeth into the man's fleshy back end to the accompaniment of a very satisfying cry of pain.

His back paws were still able to touch the ground and his front paws could push against the fence. With a shake that brought a fresh howl, Rex shook his entire body in a bid to dislodge the man's grip.

Their combined weight threatened to pull the fence panel down, and Rex knew he was about to win. So it came as a great shock when the man swung the golf club he still held.

Much like Albert, he only caught a glancing blow, the man unable to swing with any accuracy while trying to hold on to the fence. Regardless, the shock of it was enough to make Rex open his mouth. Losing his grip, he fell to the ground, and before he could gather himself to leap again, the man clambered up and over.

His right shoulder was numb where the blunt weapon struck, but Rex refused to let that stop him. Getting over the fence required a run up, but in the few seconds that took, the sound of a car starting came from the other side.

Rex gained the top of the fence in time to see a car blast away from the kerb. The scent of blood was thick in the air, he had wounded the man, but had ultimately lost the chase.

Scrambling with his back paws, he had a six-foot drop on the other side. Hitting the ground front paws first, the injury to his shoulder made itself known, Rex unable to stop the small wince of pain that left his lips.

He stayed where he was for a minute, getting his breath back and staring into the distance. The car was long gone, taking off at a speed he could never hope to match, not even on a good day.

Testing his right front leg, Rex huffed at the sharp sting he felt in his shoulder. He wasn't cut. He wasn't even that badly hurt, but running at full speed was going to be difficult for a few days. Pushing the pain down, for he had no time for it, he began to trot. He didn't want to go back over the fences to retrace his steps back to his human, but believed he could navigate around the houses to find him.

Albert was sitting up, propped against the side of a car by the time Rex reappeared. His head was bleeding from a cut behind his left ear. Using his phone he'd been able to take a picture of the wound. It wasn't bad, which is to say he didn't think it would need to be stitched to keep it closed. He'd been lucky, Albert knew that; whatever he'd been hit with was supposed to take his head off.

There was something else though. He'd been specifically targeted. This wasn't a random mugging, his attacker, whoever he or she was, hadn't been after money, so they were trying to kill him, take him out of the picture by putting him in hospital, or just plain trying to scare him off.

That told him he was making someone very nervous, but it wasn't Captain Allard because he'd left him at the field with the second body.

Or was it him?

With Rex padding down the street in his direction, Albert shifted his feet to get up and thought about the last few hours. Captain Allard threatened him in the café. Now, just a few hours later, he was on the floor and bleeding. Coincidence? Albert doubted it very much. A squeal of pain echoed through the night more than a minute earlier which told Albert Rex had caught the assailant. He was also able to tell it was a man from the sound of his pain-filled shout.

Captain Allard had sons in the police under his command and they were not all currently at the field. Any one of them could have been sent to remove the fly from the police chief's ointment.

Another thought struck him as he levered himself off the ground. He'd just outright accused the Swedish archaeologists of lying, called them out to make it clear he was on to them. They were never in the frame for killing Bjorn, but were they willing to hurt someone to protect their secrets? Had Peter or Lars chased after him to deliver the blow that came so close to punching his ticket?

Rex nuzzled into Albert, making sure his human was doing all right.

"*You're bleeding*," he pointed out, knowing even as he did that the old man wouldn't understand him. "*You seem okay though. Can we get my dinner now?*"

Food always made everything better.

Albert checked Rex over and found the spot where he was hurt when he touched it and Rex winced. Carefully lowering himself to place one knee on the pavement, he looked into Rex's eyes.

"You're hurt. Did he get you too?"

Rex rewarded Albert with a rough tongue to the chin.

His dog seemed okay, and Albert was tired, weary, and cold. The wound to the back of his head required a plaster as an absolute minimum, so with a grunt of effort, he used the car he'd been leaning against to get back to his feet. It wasn't far to their guesthouse, but he chose to take the long route rather than cut through the dark alley Celeste directed him to when he set off that morning.

Wobbling slightly, the big question in Albert's head was whether he could make it back to the guesthouse, and the sense of relative safety it would give, without suffering a second attack.

Chapter 19

"I don't think you understand the potential rewards at stake," Lars remarked. "Either one of you. Are you really going to just up and leave? What will you tell him when he asks why you failed?"

Julienne felt like an emotional wreck. She was ready to quit when she discovered Bjorn's body. That was bad enough and sufficient reason to ditch the job so far as she was concerned. Lars convinced her to stay though. It was all about risk and reward in his mind, but getting murdered was not expected to be among the potential pitfalls.

One of their team was dead for goodness sake. Now there was a body in one of the test trenches they dug to make it look like they really were conducting an archaeological survey, and it appeared as though the police were involved somehow.

They had to be. Why else would their boss have classified Bjorn's broken skull an accident?

No, it was time to go.

"But you can't," argued Lars. "We took a contract. We are expected to produce results."

Peter shook his head, his lips pursed and his eyes trained straight ahead rather than at Lars when he said, "I don't care. This is not what we signed on for. We should have found it by now. We have been looking for a week. So either it was never here, and the map was marked wrong, someone found it years ago by accident, or it is buried too deep for our equipment to find. If the last of those is the case, we will need an excavator to remove the top metre of soil. At least. But no matter what the case, La Obrey is too hot right now. Do you really think we can continue to search under our current circumstances?"

Julienne said, "Peter's right," her voice a whisper. "The police will be hovering over our dig site for a day or more as they look for evidence, and they will have questions for us. The right time to leave is now."

Lars almost started shouting, but a voice at the back of his head made him stop. It would be futile for a start; he could tell Julienne and Peter were going to leave regardless of what argument he presented. However, their departure provided an opportunity. Doing it all alone would be far harder, backbreaking even, but with the team reduced from four to one, if he found it, he would get the whole of the team's cut.

Nodding to show he accepted the wisdom of their decision, even as he laughed inwardly at their cowardly foolishness, Lars said, "You're right. You should go. I will deal with our employer, don't worry about that part. Go now if you wish, get your things and leave La Obrey. I will drive the van and rendezvous with you later."

Peter thanked him and Julienne even kissed his cheek. They both wished him luck and were gone within thirty seconds of his suggestion that they should waste no more time discussing it.

He waited until they were out of sight before leaving the van. He wanted to speak with the police before he left.

Chapter 20

"Celeste?" Albert called out stumbling through the front door of the guesthouse. His handkerchief was stained red, but not dripping wet. He held it pressed against the back of his skull where his wound stung.

His shoulder was numb where the weapon connected, but his left arm was still functional, much to his surprise.

He shuffled along the corridor in search of the landlady, trusting that she would have a first aid kit to hand. He didn't need to go to a hospital and had no desire to see a doctor, but his head would continue to bleed for some time, making a mess unless he could convince someone to apply a dressing.

"Celeste?" he called out again. It was too early to worry about waking her other guests, but he worried she might be out until he heard her voice echoing through the building.

"Mr Smith is that you? Is everything all right?"

Albert reached the dining room where guests took their breakfast each morning. There he slumped into a chair, the hand with the handkerchief still pressing against the wound.

"Well, not exactly," he provided a cryptic response, certain she would see for herself very soon.

Celeste arrived a few moments later, sweeping into the dining room with her usual bustling energy. Her eyes found Albert, and a half second later, the reason for his calls.

She swore in French, hurrying to see.

"Oh Albert, what happened? Did you fall?"

Albert chuckled, "Yes. But only after someone hit me on the head."

Celeste was hovering over her guest, her hands moving to inspect the wound when she pulled back to look in his eyes.

"Someone did this to you?" The elderly landlady sounded as though she could not believe it.

Albert didn't want to nod his reply. The numb feeling in his shoulder was forging a path to the wound in his head, giving his neck a stiffness that challenged any desire he might have to move it. Choosing not to question how bad it might be in the morning, he answered Celeste's question as honestly as he could.

"This was an attack. Someone, a man I am fairly certain, waited in ambush."

Celeste gasped, her face white with shock.

"I believe the intention was to kill me."

Celeste swore in French again, her hands wringing in front of her body. Albert had to lean back to look up at her face; tilting his neck was not an option he wished to explore.

"*I bit him*," revealed Rex. "*But he got away*," he added with a whine of disappointment.

Misinterpreting Rex's sounds, Albert used his free hand to ruffle the fur around his neck.

"Don't worry, Rex, it's just a bonk on the head. I'll be fine." The statement brought him nicely around to the reason for attracting his landlady's attention. "I don't suppose you could help me dress it, could you? It's a little difficult to see on the back of my head."

Snapped back to the present by Albert's request, Celeste jolted as though poked with a live electrical wire.

"Yes, of course. I'll fetch the first aid kit. Please give me a moment."

She bustled away, a torrent of French trailing in her wake.

With her gone, Albert thought about what he ought to do next. Telling her he was attacked had probably been a mistake. She would expect him to call the police. She might even do it for him, but was there any point in reporting the crime? Albert thought it to be about even odds that the attacker was a member of the local police whose actions were ordered by Captain Allard himself.

It was too late now for him to change what Celeste knew, but it wasn't as though he had seen his assailant's face. He couldn't provide a description even if he wanted to.

Rex was on the floorboards by Albert's feet. There was something stuck between two of his teeth and it was bothering him. Try as he might, rasping at it with his tongue was having no effect, and he couldn't get his paws at the right angle to do anything either.

Waiting for Celeste to return, Albert noticed what Rex was doing.

"Hey, Rex. You need a hand there?"

Rex looked up, his tongue lolling out of his mouth on the right side to provide a perfect pink backdrop to the strip of dark fabric jammed between his canine tooth and the premolar behind it.

"*Would you be a pal and pick that out for me, please?*" Rex whined, nudging Albert's free hand.

Albert had to squint to see and after three attempts with just his right hand, gave up and brought his left into play too. His left arm had been up behind his head for the last five minutes where he was pressing his handkerchief to soak up the blood. Albert rolled his shoulder, coaxing life back into the limb before using it to grip Rex's snout.

"*Ooo you oh ot you are doing?*" Rex managed to ask, his words garbled by the human hand inside his mouth.

Albert had to take the strip of cloth back into Rex's mouth to get it to come free, his dog almost retching in the half second before he pulled it clear.

Rex licked his teeth. "*Merci beaucoup.*"

Albert held the soggy piece of cloth between two fingers. Pleasant it was not, but as clues went it was more than nothing. The material felt and looked like hopsack; a heavy cloth used in men's trousers. He had a couple of pairs made from the same thing.

It wasn't the type of material employed in a police uniform, but that didn't mean his assailant wasn't an officer in plain clothes. Of course, what he really needed was to find the trousers Rex ripped it from. Without them he had very little and doubted the man wearing them would choose to put them back in his wardrobe. More likely they were already being incinerated somewhere.

Despite that Albert chose to keep hold of the strip of cloth. His handkerchief was already in use, so he elected to simply stuff the latest clue into his trouser pocket.

Withdrawing his hand, the piece of colourful lino fell out and bounced across the floor, reminding Albert that he had it and forcing to the surface a question about whether the blow to his head might have caused a minor concussion. That was twice he'd forgotten it now and something about the object he found wedged in the buried victim's shoe made him think it could prove important.

Celeste bustled back into the room, an open first aid kit in her hands. Holding it with her left, she rummaged with her right.

"Now, I'm going to need to get a better look at that wound, Mr Smith," she remarked, her attention on the contents of the box she held.

The piece of lino was on the floorboards two feet away where it came to rest after bouncing. To get to it, he would need to hook it with a foot, and there was no way to do that without Celeste questioning what he was doing.

"Oh, good," she remarked. "It's not as bad as I feared."

"No?" Albert was pleased to hear it.

"I think you will get away with a small dressing. It could really do with a stitch or two, but am I right to assume you do not wish to go to hospital tonight?"

"Very much so. If you can put something over it so I don't leak into your pillows, I would most certainly appreciate it."

Celeste placed the first aid kit on the table next to Albert, taking from it a packet that she ripped open to reveal a pre-soaked sterilised cloth.

"This might sting a bit," she murmured right before she stabbed his wound with red hot lava. Red hot lava laced with acid, in fact.

Albert sucked in a lungful of air through teeth clenched tight shut and did so with such force he threatened to suck in his own front teeth.

"I said it might sting," Celeste remarked, as though her half second of warning ought to have been enough.

Albert knew better than to comment, further wincing and whining would only make him seem weak and would do nothing to alleviate the nest of fire ants currently attacking the back of his skull.

"There, that's got it clean at least." Celeste pushed Albert's head forward to better inspect the cut with all the care and concern an annoyed mother might employ in patching up her child's third skinned knee that week. "I just need to close it."

Wondering if she perhaps planned to use a flamethrower to cauterise the wound first, Albert was pleased when she gently placed a piece of sticking plaster over the wound. A large square of gauze followed, sealing the plaster beneath a safety layer.

The task complete, Celeste took a step back, her foot coming down on the small piece of lino.

"What have we here?" she asked, bending at the waist to pick it up.

"Oh, um, that's nothing," Albert lied. Then, thinking better of it, he chose to go with the truth. "Celeste, I'm afraid I have some rather disturbing news."

Celeste continued to stare at the piece of lino, her eyebrows wrinkling.

"Where did you get this?" she asked.

Albert's heart skipped a beat. He thought of linoleum as an out-of-date material rarely used in the modern era, but equally knew it had been very popular in the fifties, sixties, and even the seventies. The piece he found lodged in the victim's shoe was small, but big enough to show the dazzlingly colourful pattern. A pattern many might remember.

"Celeste, do you recognise it?"

Her eyes snapped up as though the question startled her, but when she spoke her voice was calm and measured.

"Recognise it? A tiny piece of old floor? Sorry, no. Where did you get it?"

He didn't want to be the one to reveal the news, but he'd already introduced the subject and he saw no reason to lie.

"A second body was found at Drucker's Field this evening. One that was buried there many years ago." He delivered the news and watched her face, curious to see what reaction might come.

Celeste nodded, her eyes on the piece of lino she held and her thoughts anywhere but in the present.

"Another body. That's terrible," she murmured.

"The piece of lino was wedged in the victim's shoe, Celeste. Are you sure you don't recognise it? It might really help to identify who he is and what happened to him."

Celeste handed the lino fragment over, placing it in Albert's upturned palm.

"You said 'victim'. You think this person was ... what? Murdered?"

"In my experience shallow graves are inhabited only by those sought out by killers. So yes, I think the man in the field was murdered. The coroner will be able to determine roughly what year he was buried, but you have lived here longer than most, Celeste. Do you recall anyone suddenly vanishing? It would have to be at least twenty years ago, possible more like thirty or even more than that."

Celeste gave a small shake of her head. "No, I'm sorry, Albert. I do not recall anything like that ever happening. You can ask around, but I believe you will hear the same from everyone else." Turning away, she reloaded the first aid box and when she closed it, casually asked, "Are the police aware?"

"Of the body? Yes. I was with one of their officers when the discovery was made."

The answer seemed to satisfy her and she picked up the first aid kit, holding it by the handle in her right hand.

"Would you like an aspirin or something stronger? I think I have some over-the-counter painkillers to hand."

Albert said, "No, thank you. I have some in my room if I want one."

Celeste withdrew, expressing her hope that Albert would recover quickly and insisting that he should contact her in the night if he felt at all unwell.

He promised to do so, quite certain there would be no cause for such measures, and when she was gone, he questioned why she hadn't asked him more about his attacker and why it might be that she didn't suggest calling the police.

Chapter 21

An hour later in his room on the first floor, Albert had stripped down to his underwear and was inspecting the bruising on his left shoulder. He could roll it and lift his arm, which were both good signs, but wasn't fooling himself into believing it wouldn't hurt in the morning. The bruising was already visible; indicating how bad it was, and he expected to find that part of his body stiff when he woke.

He could take some painkillers and would, but whether they did much to help was debatable. Pushing his shoulder to one side while reminding himself he needed to be thankful it wasn't much worse, Albert turned his attention to his clothes.

Were they ruined or not? The cuffs of his trousers were dirty from traipsing across the field and climbing into the trenches, but they would clean up just fine. His shirt, though, had blood on the collar and that was going to be harder to get out.

Laundry had been his late wife's domain, but that wasn't to say he couldn't work the washing machine and didn't understand the need to soak and wash the blood out before it stained.

Wearing nothing but socks and his underwear, he stood at the sink in his room, scrubbing his shirt collar. All he had was soap and his fingernails – he didn't much fancy using his toothbrush to abrade the fibres – but the blood was only just dry and came out easily enough.

Hanging it up to dry on the towel rail, he was surprised to hear a knock at his door.

"Albert? Are you there?" Margot's voice cancelled his intention to ask who his caller might be, but did nothing to alleviate the need to find clothes.

Rex slid off the bed and bounded to the door, wagging his tail and sniffing at the bottom gap. He wasn't supposed to be on the bed anyway, but with his human in the bathroom he'd chosen to ignore that rule. Now the old man would never know.

"Um, just a minute," Albert replied, looking around frantically. He really needed to get some of his clothes washed. Should he put today's dirty trousers back on? Or would he be better off breaking out a new pair ready for tomorrow? He had to carry everything with him, so travelled light and that meant a limited wardrobe.

"Can I come in, Albert?" Margot asked, trying the door handle.

Seeing it turn sent a bolt of panic through Albert's heart. It wasn't so much that he was embarrassed to be nearly naked in front of another person, he would wear less at the swimming pool without giving it a second thought, but an old man's meat and two veg hidden behind loosely fitting cotton was not a sight he wished to indelibly etch into the young French woman's mind.

The door was locked, of course, Margot stuck the other side until he unlocked it.

"I'm just getting dressed," he called out, the words enough to make her wait.

The muddy trousers were discarded in favour of a clean pair of grey slacks - hopsack, Albert noted to himself. A light blue shirt and vee neck navy jumper completed the outfit quickly enough.

Rex danced in front of the door, keen to see the person outside so she could lavish him with her affections.

"Rex, please get your big bum out of the way," Albert had to grab his hips to stop them from moving, then step around him to get to the door. "And don't think I didn't notice that you were on the bed, dog."

Rex shot him a mystified look. Okay, so his human wasn't a terrible detective. He could even be quite perceptive sometimes – for a human. But how did he know he'd been on the bed?

"Wondering how I know, are you?" Albert enquired, reading his dog's expression correctly for once. "There's a giant dog-shaped bum print."

Rex was so busy inspecting the dent he'd left and wondering how to overcome that in the future, that he missed Albert opening the door and had to force himself between the humans to get Margot's attention.

The humans, however, were too distracted by each other.

"Margot, has something happened? Are you all right?" Albert enquired of the young police officer. She wasn't crying, yet couldn't hide the upwelling of negative emotion clouding her face.

"Nevermind me, what happened to you?" Margot replied, unable to miss the white gauze dressing plastered to Albert's skull.

Albert backed away, holding the door so he reversed with it in an arc to give Margot room to enter.

"Shall we exchange stories?" he suggested. "You go first."

His room had a small wooden table and two matching wooden chairs arranged in front of a window. They sat there, drinking coffee from the kettle and accompaniments supplied as they explained what each had missed when they were apart.

"I am suspended from work pending an investigation," Margot revealed with a sad sigh.

"Because you continued to look into Bjorn Ironfoundersson's death?" Albert guessed.

"Officially, it's because I disobeyed a direct order, but yes, I think you have it right. Captain Allard kept asking me what you were doing? Why you were in La Obrey and why I was with you? He seemed nervous."

A snort of amusement left Albert's nose at her claim.

"Nervous, huh? Well, someone sure is." He turned his head to give Margot a better look at the dressing stuck to the back of it. "I got this on my way back here. I didn't see who it was or what they tried to hit me with, but I believe their intention was to kill me."

"*It was a man,*" supplied Rex. "*He smelled of brandy, garlic, and cigarettes.*" Rex could have broken down the man's scent profile into more than a hundred different smells, but knew the humans wouldn't understand him.

Using the table to lever himself upright – most of his body ached from the effort of the day and he yearned for a bath – Albert went to the bedside table to the right, not the left, that was always Petunia's side. From the thin top drawer, he removed the strip of cloth and the piece of lino.

"Rex chased the guy," Albert showed her the chunk of trouser cloth, "and I'm fairly sure he bit him. He came back with this lodged between his teeth."

Margot held the still soggy piece of dark grey cloth. "Bit him? Like on the leg?" She had a thoughtful expression.

"Probably his backside," Albert chuckled, ruffling Rex's fur much to the dog's delight. "That's his preferred target. Not sure why, but he has a slightly vindictive streak."

Drawing in a deep breath of realisation, Margot's eyes flared. "Curtis was limping when he arrived at the field. I was just leaving and after five minutes of Captain Allard shouting in my face I didn't feel like asking what had happened to him."

"Curtis?"

"Yes, he's one of the Allards. Captain Allard's youngest son." She sounded angry. "I bet it was him. I've never trusted Curtis."

Frowning a little, Albert said, "I thought you only joined the police a few months ago."

"Yes, but I've lived in La Obrey all my life. He dated my eldest sister for a while about ten years ago and they broke up when she caught him with Shannon Toulouse."

"Ah." Albert didn't feel the subject needed further comment. "So he was limping. What time would that have been?"

Margot glanced at the clock on the wall. "Less than an hour ago. I saw him just before I left Drucker's Field to come here."

That meant he'd had plenty of time to have his wound patched and change his ruined trousers. It didn't mean he was guilty, but certainly made him worthy of further investigation.

"Then there is this." Albert showed her the piece of lino. "I found that lodged in the victim's shoe."

"And you took it?" Margot was incredulous, her tone suggesting he'd committed a terrible crime.

Albert was unrepentant. "I most certainly did. This could be an important clue and, you'll have to forgive me, but I don't exactly trust the police in these parts."

"No, that's fair. Good point. So it was stuck in his shoe?"

"That's right. Kind of in the back by the heel, like it might have got stuck there when someone dragged the body across the floor."

Margot stared at the fragment of lino in her hand. "You're saying this might have come from the house in which he was killed."

"I am."

"That's a start for sure. If he was killed in La Obrey."

"Buried so close to the village, I would be willing to bet money he met his end here. If we knew when, that would help, but not as much as knowing who he is."

"Then let's hope he still had his wallet in his pocket." Margot's final remark highlighted a pertinent point. Leaving ID on the victim would be sloppy in the extreme, and depending on how long ago the murder took place, there was a distinct chance there would be no dental records.

They both knew naming the victim was likely to prove difficult, but he sat firmly at the centre of the mystery surrounding Bjorn Ironfoundersson's death and it went without saying that they had to solve one case to have any hope of figuring out the other.

Chapter 22

They waited until midnight to meet, all of them sneaking from their houses in the dead of night to gather as they had before in the wine cellar beneath the village hall. They were safe there, no one would hear what they were choosing to discuss in secret, but their paranoia dictated they left a guard in the shadows outside, nevertheless.

Celeste rung her hands, unable to keep them still. She had been one of the first to arrive, desperate to speak to someone else about the news. News she told herself would never come. Until the Swedish team applied to dig in Drucker's Field, that is.

Captain Allard was last to arrive, staging it that way because the discussion couldn't start without him, and he took every opportunity to bolster his dominant position in the community.

Nervous chatter greeted his entrance.

"Let us be calm, my friends," he smiled as though there was nothing to worry about.

"Calm?" questioned Hugo. He'd changed his clothes from the day and had been in his pyjamas when the news reached his ears. "How can we be calm? Is this not everything we feared?"

"Yes, it is," Captain Allard agreed, "but it is also an opportunity."

"Opportunity?" echoed Celeste, barely able to believe her ears.

"Indeed." Captain Allard came to her, clasping her clammy hands in his. "There is no need to fret. Instead, we should rejoice. Too long have we feared his body might one day be discovered. Now it has, we can dare to draw a breath."

Hugo shook his head as though trying to clear it. "But the body, Maxwell, the cause of death cannot be hidden or falsified the way you did with the Swedish man. The medical examiner will know he was murdered and what will you do then? You will have to investigate it?"

"Yes, Hugo, that is right, I will. And what do you think will be the result of my long, drawn out, convoluted investigation? Do you think I will find the killer? This is a local matter for local police." He let the remark hang heavy in the air before pointing out, "I control the local police."

Hugo was far from satisfied, and his voice wasn't the only dissenting one in the room. Elgar, the ageing owner of Florian's Bar had a point to make.

"Do you, Maxwell? Do you control them all? I heard you had to suspend Margot Dubois this evening. She's working with that English chap staying in Celeste's place, isn't she?"

Celeste closed her eyes and wished she could block out the argument.

"She was," Captain Allard admitted. "But I doubt she will continue to do so, not if she wants to keep her job."

"And the others?" Elgar persisted. "Not every member of the local police is one of your kids. What if they question why their captain is hogging the whole investigation when he ought to be delegating it to them? What if they decide to ask a few questions of their own?"

"Then they will swiftly find themselves out of a job!" Captain Allard roared, his voice reaching full volume to beat down anyone who wished to question his ability to manage the latest threat to their secret. Seeing Celeste flinch and then quiver, he softened his voice again. "I will delegate to my sons. There is no reason to fear an uprising from the junior ranks of my force."

"And what of the old man and his dog?" The question came from a corner of the room where Janice Descartes leaned again a wall. Small in stature and grey of hair, she had been regarded as a stunning beauty in her youth. Now closing on eighty, she was still magnificent to behold, but the line of suitors had dwindled. "You know who he is, do you not?"

All eyes swung to see Captain Allard's response. With the entire room looking his way, five faces waiting to hear what he had to say, he felt on the spot and under pressure for the first time since arriving.

"Yes, I know who he is. I gave him fair warning earlier today." He tried hard to sound confident, assuring them with his relaxed smile that everything was taken care of.

"Was that before or after he found the body?" Elgar shot back.

Hugo joined in, "Your warning didn't work, Max. He left my place a few minutes after you and must have met up with Margot straight after that. What are you going to do about him?"

Celeste gasped. "Was it you who tried to have him killed earlier?"

Multiple voices reacted to her question by exclaiming, "What?"

Raising his hands to ask for calm, Captain Allard met the accusing eyes of those around him.

Hugo didn't wait for him to speak. "Did you also kill the archaeologist? This is not what we agreed!"

"I have not attacked anyone," Captain Maxwell Allard replied calmly. "I uphold the laws of this great nation, I do not defy them."

"But you just falsified the verdict of a man who we all know was murdered."

Captain Allard's lips twitched, responses almost making it into the open before being rejected.

Interrupting the challenge to his leadership and saving him in many ways, though that was not her intention, Celeste said, "He found a piece of lino."

Silence filled the air, no one saying a thing for two seconds before Janice sought clarity, "A piece of lino?"

"It was in Steve's shoe."

"Don't say his name," snapped Captain Allard.

Elgar tossed his arms in the air, expressing in a gesture, the futility of their situation.

"He's going to figure it out, Maxwell."

Captain Allard narrowed his eyes and lowered his voice until it was a darkness-filled growl, "Then we shall just have to take care of him."

Chapter 23

Albert woke himself every time he moved in the night. His left shoulder was uncomfortable though the painkillers he took kept the worst of it at bay. His head was as bad, though he'd expected it to be worse.

Despite all that, he managed to rack up enough sleep to not feel too terrible when the clock dictated it was time to get up. Never a fan of winter, the darkness outside and cold temperatures beyond the warm embrace of his covers, proved almost enough to make him roll over. Had he not hurt so much, he might have done so, but the day begged his attention and there was much to be done.

Margot hadn't stayed long, but coached his need to be wary. The village possessed a malignant force, a person willing to kill. Their failed attempt against Albert could easily spawn a second attack, and to that end Albert slept with a chair under the doorhandle.

Rex suffered none of his human's troubles or worries. He had no sense that they were in any particular danger, for had he done so, Rex would have chosen to sleep with his teeth facing the door. Woe betide anyone foolish enough to try to get to the old man with harmful intent.

Waking when Albert swung his legs off the bed, Rex yawned and stretched. He wandered across to his water bowl, draining it to slake his thirst which placed extra tension on his already full bladder. Needing to go outside, he went to the door, looking pointedly at it and then back at his human until the old man got the message.

"Yes, yes, I get it," Albert hurried to deal with his own pressing bathroom needs and don some clothes. He could brush his teeth and tidy himself properly after Rex had been outside. Only when Albert reached for the chair beneath the handle did he think to question if an early morning walk in the dark was safe or not.

"Can we get a move on?" Rex whined. *"I really need to be outside."*

Telling himself it was highly unlikely anyone would choose to target him twice in twelve hours, and hopeful last night's attacker still sported a rather sore bottom, Albert removed the chair and opened the door.

No mad axe-wielding form filled the frame, and the guesthouse was as quiet as could be. Until Rex thundered down the stairs that is. Albert found him huffing and panting by the front door. Clipping his lead, but keeping the handle loose in his hand in case he did need to let him go in a hurry, Albert stepped out into the cold.

And it really was cold.

And snowing.

Rex blinked, his eyes almost crossing when a fat flake landed on the tip of his nose. They fell on his ears too, each one causing an involuntary twitch.

Albert swore under his breath. The streetlamps illuminated the snow as it fell, a light breeze causing it to swirl. Less than an inch had fallen, but the sky promised more. The locals knew to expect it; they even said it was late. Albert would have preferred to leave the village before the winter weather hit, but it was too late for that now.

Taking care to be sure his boots didn't slip, he stepped out into the street. Rex needed exercise, but showing how keen his need had been he was already marking the wall where he stood.

They didn't venture far, Albert choosing a route just long enough to be sure Rex had been given time enough to do what was necessary.

Coming back into the guesthouse, Albert stamped his boots hard to remove the snow on the mat and when he looked up, he found Celeste watching him from down the hall. She was dressed for the day with thick boots on her feet and an apron around her waist. The scent of freshly baked bread and coffee filled the house to show that her day had started several hours earlier.

"Good morning, Albert. Did you sleep well? How is your head this morning?"

"Good morning, Celeste. I slept perfectly well, thank you," Albert chose not to burden her with his tale of constantly waking every time he moved in the night. "And I have no ill effects from the cut to my head."

The answer appeared to satisfy her curiosity and she turned back toward the kitchen saying, "Officer Dubois is waiting for you in the dining room."

Heading straight there, Albert found Margot pacing by the window.

"You're okay?" she asked the instant she saw him. Clearly his wellbeing had been troubling her.

"Quite so, yes."

"*But we're hungry,*" added Rex. "*So, let's get on with the investigation and all that, but not until we've had something to eat. The dog works better on a full stomach.*"

Margot looked down at Rex, petting his head when he wagged his tail at her.

The side door leading to the kitchen opened, Celeste stepping half a foot into the room.

"Will you be joining Mr Smith for breakfast?"

Margot shot questioning eyes at Albert.

"Have you eaten?" he enquired. It wasn't yet eight o'clock and the girl looked like she could do with a good meal.

"Um, well."

"Yes," Albert replied on her behalf. "Please put her meal on my tab."

Celeste reversed into the kitchen to Margot saying, "There's really no need …"

"It's too trivial to discuss." Albert dismissed her protestations. "Now, I had a few thoughts in the night."

Margot's eyebrows lifted.

"How is it all connected?" He guided his young companion to a table, Rex following. "Yesterday I learned the Swedish had to apply to the La Obrey council be able to conduct their dig and that their application was opposed."

"By whom?"

"Precisely," Albert replied. "We should find that out and ask them why, though I suspect the answer is because they knew there to be a body in the ground where the archaeologists were proposing to excavate."

"You still think the victim could be someone local?"

"How old are you?"

Margot hadn't expected the question but said, "I'll be twenty-six in February."

"This will have occurred before you were born. My working theory is that someone either came to town and was killed here by one of the locals or the victim *is* one of the locals. If the latter is the case, there will be people who recall someone going missing. Or abruptly leaving town without warning or notice. The body was never meant to be found and I believe there is a cover up involving several members of the village."

Trying not to frown and failing, Margot asked, "What makes you think that? The people I know are all peaceful and respectable. Murderous conspiracies do not occur here." She wasn't exactly defensive, but certainly wasn't buying into the theory either.

"What makes me think it?" Albert held up his right hand and started counting off his fingers. "Your boss covered up the murder of a Swedish archaeologist from a team whose seemingly harmless application to dig a few holes in a field was opposed. The question of why he would want to do that has now been answered: because he knew they might disturb the body. That means he is involved and that conflicts with my theory that it had to have occurred before you were born."

"But he's twice my age."

"Exactly."

Rex, disturbed by the total lack of breakfast, rose from his prone position. Sitting, his head was above the surface of the table, though his lolling tongue hung below it.

"*You appeared to have missed a vital step this morning,*" he coached Albert.

This was a situation where a translator was not necessary. Scratching Rex behind his ears, Albert said, "Sorry, boy. I'll give you some from my plate and give you a full portion of kibble when we get to the room. I can't go just now though."

Rex, hungry and not inclined to wait, sunk back to his belly and waited for the conversation above him to resume.

"Where was I?" Albert tried to recall what he'd been saying. "Oh, yes, Captain Allard is in his fifties, so he was either a very young man when the murder occurred, something we can confirm with the coroner later …"

"But I'm suspended," Margot interrupted. "I will lose my job if I go into work and start asking questions about this case."

"We'll circle back to that." Albert pressed on. "Unless Captain Allard is the killer, which I suppose he could be, he helped to cover up the murder. You might immediately want to ask why, but the more pertinent question is to do with who the killer is to him? He must know them well enough to want to protect them. Enough to risk his career, his pension, and possibly incarceration if the truth were to get out."

Margot wanted to reject what the old man sitting opposite had to say. It was ludicrous, but nothing else made sense either.

Thinking aloud, she said, "We need to ask some of the older villagers. If someone went missing, a resident, that is, they ought to remember it. Last month one of my friends found out she was pregnant and the whole village knew by the afternoon. Secrets are hard to keep here."

Albert nodded thoughtfully. It was much the same in his village in England. It was much the same in any small community for that matter. People live too close together and there are so few of them that everyone knows everyone. It led him neatly to his next point.

"Hugo at the café is also involved."

"But he's ancient," Margot protested.

Albert raised one eyebrow and waited.

Margot's cheeks flushed. "Sorry. I mean he's a lot older than Captain Allard."

"He is, but a body is a hard thing to move. It's not called a dead weight for nothing. Someone killed that poor man and they had help to cover up their crime. Our job now is to figure out the how and the why and the who. That will give us our killer. And we had better work fast before your boss finds out what we are doing. Someone tried to kill me last night and it was probably the same person who did for Bjorn Ironfoundersson. My guess would be that he is our killer and the archaeological dig on top of where he hid the body had him taking extreme steps to cover his tracks."

"But it can't be Captain Allard. The timings are wrong. He was at the crime scene when you were attacked. And it can't be any of his kids unless you are wrong about the dates. The eldest of them is only a few years older than me."

Albert shrugged. "That is why they call it investigating. We have part of a picture. Now we get to fill in the blanks."

The door from the kitchen opened again, Celeste coming through with a trolley loaded down with breads, cheeses, cold cuts, yoghurts, fruit, and more.

No one noticed the tail slipping through the gap just before the door closed.

Albert and Margot watched, patient and silent, until she had it in position next to a long table against a wall. There she offloaded the breakfast items to set up a buffet.

"Please help yourself," Celeste invited. "I'll be back in a few moments with coffee."

His stomach rumbling, for there had been very little to eat after his oversized lunch, Albert wasted no time getting to his feet.

Looking down to tell Rex he needed to 'stay' Albert found the space his dog ought to occupy mysteriously empty.

"Rex?"

A squeal of alarm from the kitchen answered his question before he could give it voice.

Chapter 24

Rex ran from the kitchen with a whole French stick between his teeth. He'd found eggs first, and knowing the delicious treat they contained, tipped three dozen of them onto the floor. The stack of eggs didn't all break on impact, but most did and his tongue made short work of the runny mess. Next he found fruit, which did not appeal, but the fresh bread smelled good. He would have taken his time, but the kitchen door opened, the landlady returning, so acting on impulse he bit hold of the nearest loaf and took off.

Albert expected better from his dog, but also knew Rex wasn't one to wait to be fed. His belly ruled his head all too often, so he should have known delaying Rex's breakfast would result in mischief.

Grabbing the kitchen door, he yanked it open just in time for Rex to rush out.

The French stick, held gently between his teeth like a prize, made it through the door without touching either side, but Albert's legs were not so lucky. Rex misjudged the gap, whacking into Albert's shins with the still-warm loaf. Bread though, is a very different beast from steel, so it snapped neatly just beyond Rex's lips. The other side collided with a chair leg, also snapping off, which left Rex holding nothing but the smallest piece in his mouth.

"*Awww, nuts*," he whined, skidding to a stop.

"Rex," Albert used his 'bad dog' voice.

Guiltily, Rex let the remaining piece of French stick drop from his mouth. It plopped stickily on to the floor leaving behind nothing more than a promise of how good it would have tasted.

Disappointed, Albert clipped Rex's lead to his collar.

"Won't be a moment," he called on his way out. He left the dining room, turned right at the stairs to climb them and leave Rex in their room to think about things. He did, of course, fill his bowl with kibble; there was no need to deny the dog food and every chance Rex would find some new and unique way to levy retribution if he did.

Back in the dining room, Albert found Margot quizzing Celeste. It was clear from the landlady's expression that she wanted to return to the kitchen, though whether that was to avoid the questions or because something might burn, he could not tell.

"What about missing people, Madam Darroze? Was there anyone you can recall who went missing from the village. Someone who just up and left one night and was never seen again? A husband perhaps?"

When Celeste offered no answer, Margot continued to prompt her memory.

"How about a rumour that a man had run off with another woman? That must have happened at some point."

Celeste looked to be scraping the bottom of her memory, but was coming up blank.

"I'm sorry, Margot, I just don't remember anything like that ever happening here. I mean, sure, there were people who left La Obrey over the years, but none I can recall who suddenly vanished." Edging toward the kitchen door, she said, "I'm really must get back. The other guests will be down soon."

Margot let her go, frowning her disappointment at Albert. "Lots of dead ends," she remarked. "Is it always like this?"

"No, not always. No two cases are the same, but I will say this one is a little perplexing. I'm still not sure how the Swedish Archaeologists fit in." Albert took a plate and began to load it with breakfast fare. "Their desire to dig up the field in which the body was hidden got them mixed up in this, but its fails to explain why their behaviour is so odd. What were they doing with metal detectors in their quest for a Stone Age settlement?"

Chapter 25

Lars had not slept well, a combination of excitement over the prospect of such a huge score, gut-wrenching doubt that he could find it, and concern regarding the logistics of recovering it by himself.

It ought to be possible and they had explored so much of the field already that the areas left to survey were small enough he believed he could manage alone. In the end it all came down to whether the map had been marked accurately enough in 1942.

Walter Karlsson, born in Sweden to a Swedish father by a German mother, had left his homeland to join the Nazis only weeks after they invaded Poland. A master of antiquities at the Vasa Museum in Stockholm, he was welcomed by the party and assigned to aid their efforts to rape Europe of its fine arts, gold, and valuables.

Yet Walter saw an opportunity in his work. He was just one of many the Nazi Party sent to manage the inventory of plunder taken from every corner of every country. It was his task to catalogue it, so who would know if slightly less than everything made it back to the Fatherland?

He didn't start out stealing it. In the beginning, he made sure to send every last scrap to the Fuhrer, but when America agreed to aid the allied nations as part of the Lend-Lease Act of 1941, Walter questioned if the mighty German machine could withstand the combined onslaught of so many opposing nations.

Thinking prudently, he began to feather his own nest. He buried gold and silver, jewels, coins, and other non-perishables in spots across Europe. Everywhere he went, he made sure to subtract a small percentage for himself.

However, the small percentages were valuable and there were so many of them. Walter knew the Nazis would never miss what they couldn't know even existed and confidently committed a crime no one would ever know about.

The war would end one way or another, and he would return a few years down the line to collect that which he had safely left behind. A map went everywhere with him, the markings on it impossible to decipher without the codes which he sent in letters to his wife in Sweden.

His plan might have come to fruition had fate not chosen to play a part.

The war did end, the allies sweeping across Europe to drive the Germans back to their own country. Ditching his uniform and switching from speaking German to Swedish, he had no trouble making his way north. On the one occasion he was questioned, he was able to show his credentials as a scholar working at the Vasa Museum.

Once home, Walter believed all he needed to do was wait. Let a few years pass and he could return to collect the caches he left behind. Even after the cut he would lose exchanging the gold and jewels on the black market, he would be a very rich man. A very rich man indeed.

But before he could make it back to his house, his wife, and his young son, Walter stepped out in front of a baker's truck. His head too full of dreams to notice its approach, his fate was sealed before the horrified baker could wrestle his vehicle to a stop.

Walter died on a back road in Stockholm staring up at the sky with a shocked look on his face.

Almost eighty years later, when his son died, Walter's map and the letters he sent his wife were among the many items bequeathed to a grandson he would never meet.

Lars knew only a tiny fraction of the story, enough that he knew what he was after and where the map coordinates came from. His employer assured him his grandfather listed everything that was buried at each site, but Lars doubted that was true. Rather, he believed it was a lie concocted to stop the people sent to recover the plundered loot from keeping some back for themselves.

Exactly as Walter had.

Well, Lars was going to take some anyway. He was getting the full share for the team – provided he could find the spot where Walter Karlsson buried it – and why shouldn't he take a little extra for his troubles? Without his determination to see the task through, his employer would get nothing from this spot.

The police were still here though, a white canvas tent erected over the hole where the body had had been found. He'd watched the victim's remains be removed just a few hours ago, the body exhumed from its muddy grave to be examined elsewhere.

He couldn't finish his search of the field until they were gone, and were he to risk it and find the spot where the cache of Nazi plunder was buried, he couldn't start to dig without someone seeing and choosing to investigate. Even if they did so out of boredom. Hauling gold bars from the ground to load was sure to be noticed.

No, he needed the police to be distracted elsewhere and he had just the idea for how to achieve that.

Chapter 26

Their breakfasts finished, Albert and Margot discussed how best to tackle the tasks on their list. It made sense to stick together – there was no question they were in danger, but to cover the most ground they also needed to split up.

Albert wanted to visit the coroner's office or, more accurately, he wanted Margot to. He would go with her, but she was going to have to break some rules if they hoped to get answers. Curtis required some investigation. Turning up with a convincing limp so soon after Rex bit someone wasn't enough to colour him as guilty, but it went a long way.

"Rex might be able to identify him," Albert suggested when they had discussed it.

Margot did little to hide her scepticism. "I don't think canine line ups are admissible in court in any country, but they are certainly not allowed in France."

Rolling his eyes, Albert said, "What I mean is, he could tell me if Curtis is the man he chased."

Margot's frown deepened even further. "How exactly is he going to do that?"

"Nevermind," Albert dismissed the subject. "Just trust me. Rex is the smartest darned dog I ever met. He will find a way to let me know."

However, before they even thought about tracking down Captain Allard's youngest son, they wanted to speak with the residents of the houses whose gardens Rex chased the unknown assailant through. They might have seen something. Someone might even have a camera pointing that way; such devices were so prevalent now.

Also on the list was the urgent need to find out who opposed the Swedish application to excavate Drucker's Field. They agreed the name on that form had to be there because whoever it was knew about the body; the coincidence was too great to believe any other reason.

Overarching it all, the need to keep their investigation hidden from the police and anyone else who might be involved – difficult when they couldn't guess who knew about the body – could not be ignored. They were going to have to step carefully and no mistake.

"Ready? Margot asked.

Albert aimed his feet at the stairs. "I'll just fetch Rex."

Rex was on the bed. To his way of thinking, he was already in the old man's bad books for stealing the bread and making a mess in the kitchen, so having a doze on the soft, spongey mattress couldn't make things any worse.

He heard Albert approaching anyway, his ears attuned enough to recognise the sound and cadence of his human's footsteps. Coming down off the bed, Rex checked the covers. His human made the bed neat when he got out of it, a habit Rex found just as odd as the rest of human behaviour. Now a distinct divot showed where he'd been resting.

Taking one edge of the covers between his teeth, Rex gently tugged, making the surface flat once more. Wagging his tail at his own ingenuity, Rex spun around and sat looking obedient and happy when the door opened inward.

Albert narrowed his eyes. Rex never sat in the middle of the room like a good boy. Like a child out of sight in another room, whose parent knows to be suspicious when they go quiet, Albert knew something was amiss.

"*Hello,*" Rex wagged his tail. "*Sorry about earlier. I got hungry.*"

Albert looked about, his hands finding their way to his hips.

"What have you been up to this time?"

Rex's eyebrows performed a little dance as he deciphered the questions.

"*I have no idea what you mean.*" His face portrayed angelic innocence.

Albert checked the bathroom and under the bed, but finding no sign of damage, destruction, or mischief of any kind, he ruffled the fur around Rex's neck. He could never stay mad at him for long and blamed himself for the breakfast theft – he should have dealt with Rex's needs first. Maybe that's not how a dog trainer would say things should work, but Rex was more partner than pet.

"Come on, boy. We've a day ahead of us." Rex bounded forward through the door, sneaking a look back at the bed. It was a trick to remember.

Downstairs they found Margot waiting and as they were heading for the guesthouse's front door, Celeste appeared.

"Albert?" she called to delay his exit. When he turned to face her, she said, "You were originally booked for two nights. Do you intend to extend your stay?"

She sounded neither hopeful nor ready to tell him new guests were arriving and he would need to leave.

"Oh, yes, sorry. I'd rather forgotten to discuss that with you."

"I have a spare room if you need it," Margot volunteered.

"No, no," Celeste jumped in quickly, too quickly perhaps, her need to stave off Margot's offer sounding urgent. "I merely wish to check Mr Smith will still be here tonight. Otherwise I will need to strip his bed and remake it for the next guest."

"Thank you, Celeste. I will require another night at least. Will that be a problem?" Albert wasn't sure when he would leave now. His next destination awaited, but he hadn't bothered to book a room. It was low season and he felt confident there would be plenty of places with rooms available.

"No problem at all," she replied.

Spotting something, Albert hesitated before saying, "You have a ... um. There's some thread hanging from your sleeve."

Celeste wore a pale cream woollen jumper over a long cotton skirt. Snagged on her left arm, right by her elbow where she might not notice it all day, was a length of dark green thread.

Celeste tried to look where Albert pointed, but watching the poor woman lift her arm and stretch her neck, he chose to go to her rescue, much as he would for his wife. No one wanted to walk around with fluff, thread, or marks on their clothes.

Albert caught the offending strand between two fingers, lifting it clear.

"Thank you, Albert," Celeste held out her hand to take it. "I needed to darn a sock earlier."

Handing it over, Albert bade her good day and followed Margot from the building where the snow had stopped falling. As it always does, the unblemished, pure white coating had transformed their surroundings.

The village was a picturesque place anyway, but the snow was making it extra special. It reminded Albert of skiing holidays. However, when they got to the pavement, Rex stopped moving.

His nose was up, his ears were alert, and his hackles were raised. Albert saw all this because his right arm was attached his dog, and neither were going anywhere.

Rex sniffed deeply. It was the same scent. The man from last night, the man from the park. Growling quietly, he put his nose to the ground and started to track.

Chapter 27

"What is it, Rex?" Albert knew his dog was following a scent; this was far from the first time he'd done it.

Rex kept his eyes forward and his nose close to the ground, unwilling to be distracted when he replied, "*The man who attacked you last night. I think I might bite him again. And this time I won't let go.*"

Margot looked impatient to get where they were going, but she followed when Albert said, "He's onto something," and hurried in the opposite direction with Rex at the end of his lead.

Annoyingly faint because of the snow, the scent still hung in the air. It was mixed with blood, which made Rex curious to find out why. It was definitely the same man, the profile of the smell was spot on, just with the addition of blood. He'd bitten him and punctured his flesh, but that was hours ago. Unless he was injured far worse than Rex imagined, it made no sense for the blood smell to remain.

Old blood, Rex decided, getting a better hit.

Trailing behind his dog, Albert wondered where they could be going. There were no footsteps, the path ahead of them a blanket of pristine white crystals. Could Rex follow a scent that was under the snow?

Rex surged onward; the smell was growing in strength and that meant he was getting closer. In fact, he was starting to question if he might find the man lying in the snow somewhere ahead. Blood, more than anything, filled his nostrils and it was anything but fresh.

Had his bite somehow injured the man so badly he'd bled out? Was he about to find a body? Rex felt no emotion either way. Killing a human definitely fell into the 'bad dog' category, but not when he was defending his human and the old man had given him the command to give chase.

Albert wanted Rex to slow down. His dog wasn't having any trouble finding purchase on the snow, but Albert's walking boots, new for the trip to Europe, were struggling to grip the street. The treads were filled with compacted white stuff to the point that he might just as well have been wearing house slippers.

"Rex," he tugged at the lead. "Rex, slow down."

But Rex increased his speed, his legs controlled by his nose which was zeroing in on the source of the smell. They hadn't gone far, no more than forty yards from the front door of Celeste's guesthouse, to where the alley cut through between the houses.

They had walked the route several times now, only avoiding it last night when Albert deemed it prudent to stick to well lit paths, a strategy that led them right into the killer's path.

Angling between the houses, Rex stopped. The scent was gone. Backtracking a few paces, he nudged at the snow with his nose, exposing a bloody cloth. Coated in snow, it appeared to be nothing more than a piece of litter lying in the street, and had his nose not found it, the object might have laid there for days, weeks, or even months, depending on how long the snow lasted.

Rex looked at Albert, then meaningfully back at the bloody rag before pawing gently at the snow.

A little out of breath, Albert gave himself a moment, then asked, "What have you got there, Rex?"

"*The killer's blood.*" Rex was disappointed it wasn't more ... that it wasn't the man himself. Not that he needed to prove his ability for the sake of his ego. Whether the police caught him, or the dog had to step in and save the day didn't matter too much so long as he never got another chance to hurt his human.

He looked around and sampled the air, but the bloody rag was all there was to find.

Albert reeled Rex in a little. He could see Rex's find – a handkerchief. It had once been white, but much of it was now stained a deep, dark crimson where blood had dried into the material.

"Hey, Margot?" He wanted her to come closer. "Got a baggie or something in one of your pockets?"

"A baggie?" she repeated, unfamiliar with the term.

Albert was down in a crouch, his right knee almost but not quite touching the snow. It would have been more comfortable to use it for support on the ground, but that would mean getting a wet knee.

"I have something here." When she came closer, he showed her.

Margot had never owned a dog and wasn't what one might label a 'dog' person. Essentially, she was indifferent to the species though she got that some were very cute and some could be employed for their superior sense of smell. The La Obrey Police did not have a canine section and she had never seen a police dog in action save for on a video at the academy.

However, she recognised the significance of a bloody rag so soon after Albert's attack and so close to where it happened.

Producing a latex glove from a pocket of her coat, she nudged Albert to one side and picked it up. It was frozen solid, the liquid in the blood making the material keep its shape when she lifted it. Upending it removed most of the snow to show that while it was soaked with blood, it wasn't of a volume that would indicate a terrible wound.

Of course, Albert claimed Rex probably bit his assailant's backside and that part of the body is mostly flesh and doesn't bleed much.

"Are those initials?" Albert came in close, driven by his excitement. Had they just found a worthwhile clue.

Embroidered into the white cotton were two letters: C.D.

"Celeste Darroze," Margot murmured the name, looking back down the street towards the guesthouse.

"That's a man's handkerchief," Albert pointed out.

Margot levied one raised eyebrow at her elderly companion. "You think women all have silk handkerchiefs?"

Albert chose not to answer. Petunia's handkerchiefs had been feminine even though they were cotton, not silk. Regardless, the initials could match up to a dozen other individuals in La Obrey for all he knew and even if it was Celeste's, that didn't tell them anything. She could have suffered a nosebleed days ago. The handkerchief might have gone out with the trash but blown away on a breeze.

Hearing the humans argue about it, Rex hung his head in disappointment. " *That's a man's blood,*" he clarified, not that the humans understood or even acknowledged his comment. "*Surely, even with your pathetic noses, you can tell the difference.*" They couldn't though and he found himself feeling sympathy for their handicap.

Using Margot's glove as a makeshift bag, Albert tucked the item away for later consideration. There were tests the police could do to determine the identity of the blood but only against other samples to see if it matched. Most likely, the handkerchief would prove useless as a piece of evidence, but one never could tell.

Passing back in front of the guesthouse all three turned to give it a suspicious inspection, Albert and Margot with their eyes, Rex with his nose, checking for any indication the man he sought might have been there.

Arriving back at the site where Albert received his blow to the head, a clear rectangle of road showed where a car had once been. Close to the kerb, a few spots of dried blood told the tale of his attack.

Rex sniffed at them, unhappy his human's blood got spilled when he was so close by. He expected to be able to prevent such incidents.

"Where was he?" Margot asked. She had her back to the road and her face aimed at the garden wall.

"Up there," Albert pointed to a gap between two shrubs. The garden sat three feet above the street with the fence extending a further three feet above that. It was a great place for an ambush. A person would need only to crouch to become completely invisible. Popping up at the last moment, they would have height advantage on top of the element of surprise.

Albert was evidence of that; he never saw his attacker before or after he swung the blow that almost cracked his skull.

Margot continued up the street. "Let's knock and see if Emma is home."

"You know who lives here?" Albert questioned.

"It's a small village," she replied without turning around, her purposeful strides carrying her to the front door of the house.

Albert couldn't decide whether to be impressed or not. He also lived in a small village. Not as small as La Obrey, but not much bigger either, and he didn't know everyone.

A shadow appeared behind the frosted glass of the window a few moments after Margot rang the doorbell. It came closer, materialising into the form of a woman in her early sixties when she opened the door.

She wore thinly framed spectacles, a pink sweater with a picture of kittens playing on the front, and purple trousers with stitched creases down the front.

"Margot?" She was surprised to see the young police officer on her doorstep. Perhaps not least because she was in plain clothes. Twitching her eyes to take in the older man standing behind her, the lady of the house was about to question the visit when Margot got in first.

"Hello, Emma, I wonder could I have a look at your garden and ask a few questions?"

Emma's eyebrows wiggled in question. "My garden?"

A minute later they were looking at some crushed shoots coming up through her soil. They were protected from the worst of the snow by a shrub that bordered the fence.

"They were growing nicely yesterday," Emma complained, wandering back to her house to fetch a dustpan and brush at Margot's request.

Margot used it to clear away the snow. The ground beneath was frozen, though only right on the surface – the cold had not yet penetrated any deeper than that, but it was enough to have preserved a pair of boot prints.

Plant murder aside, Emma was shocked to hear of Albert's attack.

"Someone was in my garden?"

"I'm afraid so." Margot looked at the garden gate. It led to the street via some short steps and made accessing the back of Emma's house about as easy as any criminal might want it to be. "I don't suppose you heard or saw anything, did you?"

Emma had not, nor had anyone else in the row of houses. Not that every resident was in, but their knocks were answered by enough people to feel confident the rest would also lead to dead ends.

Albert's attacker, whoever he was, hadn't left much behind save for the shoe prints. Margot recorded the size and took photographs, but suspended from work there wasn't much else she could do.

However, in the last garden of the row, Albert noticed Rex staring at the fence. It was higher than all the others in the street, standing a shade over six feet tall so Albert could not see over it. Getting onto his tiptoes, he peered over the lip to find the pavement was at the same level as his feet.

The gardens were flat and the houses were all built at the same level, but the land fell away to the southwest hence the three-foot wall down to the pavement by the time one reached Emma's property at the far end.

Snow coated the road on the other side, except in a couple of spots where cars had pulled away to leave the bare tarmac exposed. There being nothing to see, he climbed down and a voice at the back of his head reminded him to pay attention to what Rex was doing.

It had taken him a while to notice his dog's odd behaviour, but once he did, all those months ago in Melton Mowbray when it first became apparent Rex was trying to impart some kind of message, Albert learned to watch for it. Right now, his German Shepherd was up on his back legs, both front paws dangling in the air as he tried to balance while sniffing a bush.

Albert moved in closer, tracking Rex's eyes to see what his dog might have found.

It was a piece of fluff.

Albert picked it from the thorny branch on which it had snagged. The white fibres were artificial, the kind that were used to stuff sleeping bags or the puffy style of winter coat Albert saw so many people wear these days.

Had it come from his attacker? There was no way to tell, but the white fibres were clean and springy, two things he believed would be missing had they been in the bush for very long.

He popped them into a pocket and patted Rex on the head. "Well, done, boy."

Rex wagged his tail. It wasn't always easy pointing things out to his human. To Rex the mystery man's scent was obvious and easy to find. It permeated the fibres, his sweat and general odour clinging to them.

Margot had finished up talking to Henri, the owner of this particular property, and since there didn't seem to be anything else to see, Albert clicked his tongue at Rex - it was time to move on.

Chapter 28

Their next destination was the village library. Margot assured Albert that it 'wasn't much'. It was, however, the one place they might expect to find information about the archaeological dig application and the motion to oppose it. Not because the library handled such things, but because the library also doubled as the village town hall and council offices. Anything official that happened in La Obrey was handled there according to Margot.

It sat on the eastern side of the park and when Margot described where they were going, Albert realised he'd walked past the building more than once.

The sun was out, blazing down from a bright blue sky now that the snow clouds were moving away. It made the fresh snow crystals sparkle and twinkle like diamond dust, but with an unforgiving brightness that stung Albert's eyes.

Margot fished a pair of sunglasses from her pocket, but had none to offer Albert.

"Sorry, would you like these?" she offered, seeing him squint and use a hand to shield his eyes.

Albert took one look at the overly big, rounded, black-framed and very feminine design, and said, "They're not really my style. Thank you though." From a coat pocket he fished a flat cap, positioning it low on his forehead so the meagre peak gave some shade to his eyes.

It was no more than a ten-minute walk to the library even at Albert's ambling pace, but they didn't get there.

"That's Curtis," Margot stopped abruptly and held out an arm at shoulder height to stop Albert.

Emerging from his house and limping heavily, a man resembling Captain Allard – the hair and distinctive Gallic nose gave him away – struggled to his car and gingerly bent down to take an ice scraper from the driver's door bin.

"Lazy git," Margot murmured. "It's a two-minute walk to the station."

Had Albert been more observant, he might have noticed that Rex paid the man no attention. He should have picked up on that and sensed that he could therefore not be his attacker from the previous evening. Disappointingly, he was too focused on the man in his car.

Remarking, "I might not want to walk if I had puncture wounds in my derriere," he pondered how he would confirm they had the right man. "You think he is going to work?"

Margot nodded. "Yes, I know the shift patterns. He starts at noon and likes to get in early enough to ease into his day. Also, he has a terrible relationship with his wife and spends as little time at home as possible. Stay here. I'm going to say hello and ask what happened to him. I guess he will lie, but I want to hear what he says."

Margot pointed Albert to an overgrown hedge at the edge of someone's garden. It provided perfect cover to hide him from view yet afforded the chance to observe by looking through the foliage.

Margot approached Curtis just as he got started clearing the snow off his car.

Listening intently, Albert stayed quiet.

"Hi, Curtis," Margot waved.

Not expecting anyone, Curtis spun around to see where the voice had come from.

"Oh, hi, Margot. No work for you today, I guess."

Margot arranged her face into a glum expression. "Yeah, I kinda hoped I could talk to you about that, actually. How mad is your dad?"

"Pretty mad, I guess. I haven't seen him like this before. You really ought to learn to follow orders, Margot."

Margot tried a nervously hopeful smile. "You think he's going to let me come back to work? I mean, you don't think he will fire me?"

"Fire you?" Curtis showed surprise at the suggestion. "No, I don't see why he would want to. Unless there's more to the story than I know." He put the ice scraper down and folded his arms, looking down at Margot with a superior expression. "I was told you tried to undermine the verdict on Bjorn Ironfoundersson and he caught you working with that old fart from England."

"Old fart?" Albert repeated indignantly. He'd been called a great many things in his life, but 'old fart' was a new one.

Bored, Rex sniffed at the hedge. It smelled of cats. They used the space under the hedge as an observation post to watch the street and to ambush unwitting birds when they flew into the branches above their heads.

Snorting at the odours clinging to the dirt where the snow hadn't been able to penetrate, he managed to suck a seed up his left nostril.

He sneezed violently, his face contorted to look like a bad Picasso painting.

Curtis whipped his head around, staring at the bush behind which Albert now hid, his body as still as he could make it.

Rex sneezed again, clawing at his nose in a panicked attempt to dislodge the seed.

"*Waaaaah-chooo! Arrrch, get it out!*"

Albert flared his eyes at Rex. Pointlessly because Rex wasn't looking his way.

Curtis shot Margot an accusing look. "Who is that? Is that the old fart again? Are you still working with him?" Forehead creased in anger, he limped in Albert's direction.

Cursing under his breath, Albert looked about for a place to hide. The hedge ran between two properties and if he followed it there was a garage with a path around the side. That would provide a hiding place, but the snow would show Curtis which way he had gone better than a trail of breadcrumbs.

Margot was lying vigorously, assuring Curtis she had never actually been working with the 'old fart' as he put it, but through the small gaps in the hedge, Albert could see him coming.

Rex sneezed again, his whole head shaking from one side to the other from the force of it. The seed, until then lodged deep in his left nostril where he felt convinced it was irritating his brain, chose that moment to let go. It left Rex's nose at speed along with several globs of dog snot, which all landed on Albert's trousers.

Relieved, Rex licked his nose and wagged his tail. "*That's better.*"

Albert didn't care about his dog's nose or even about the mucus adorning the shins of his clean trousers. He wanted a magical way to disappear, and when the front door of the property in which he hid began to open, he threw caution to the wind.

Now trapped between the approaching Curtis and the homeowner, Albert scooped Rex with both arms, stepped off the drive and into the snow-free dirt at the base of the hedge. Edging sideways like a crab, and with Rex giving him a 'What the heck?' face, he checked to see how close Curtis was.

Had it not been for his limp, Captain Allard's youngest son would have already rounded the hedge though Margot was doing her best to delay him.

"Hey, don't walk away from me, Curtis," she protested. "I'm trying to talk to you here. What happened to you anyway? Why are you limping so badly?"

The front door of the house swung wide, a young labrador bouncing out of it. The dog clocked Rex and Albert instantly, but held in check by a lead, all it could do was look.

"*What doing?*" it asked.

Still being carried, his paws dangling, Rex said, "*Beats me.*"

Albert wheezed, "My God you are heavy, dog. You are definitely going on a diet."

Rex swung his head around to stare at his human, knowing he'd heard correctly, but not believing his ears.

The labrador's owner was arguing with someone inside the house, only her right hand and forearm showing.

Albert reached the garage and the narrow passage leading past it to the back garden. The brief flurry of snow penetrated only a foot and a half, so with a grunt of determination, he hopped from the dirt to the paving slabs and hugged the wall.

Crouching and mercifully putting Rex down, he listened to Curtis when he answered Margot's persistent questioning.

"I twisted my ankle in the dark if you must know. That field is deadly with all the holes those stupid archaeologists have dug."

"Your ankle?" Margot questioned, looking down at it. If it was swollen, she could not tell through his trousers and thick winter boots.

The homeowner finished yelling at her partner and left the house, slamming the door in her wake.

Rex whined, "*You're not really going to restrict my food, are you? I'm already feeling hungry just worrying about it.*" He tried to lick Albert's chin.

Albert placed a hand over Rex's mouth and begged him to, "Shussssh."

The labrador tried to get around the car parked on the driveway to see the man and dog sheltering at the side of the garage.

"Where are you going, Rufus?" the woman demanded.

"*To see the man and the dog.*"

With an impatient yank, the woman dragged Rufus down the drive, obliterating Albert and Rex's footprints just a heartbeat before Curtis appeared at the bottom of her drive.

"Yes?" she snapped, in no mood to be questioned about her marital bliss.

"Good morning, Cassandra," Curtis mumbled. "Sorry, I thought I heard something."

Distracted now by different people, Rufus lunged, rising onto his back legs in a bid to get to them.

"Get down!" Cassandra growled. Aiming fierce eyes at Curtis, she snarled, "You should learn to mind your own business." Admonishment delivered, she went around both him and Margot without a second glance.

Two minutes later, Curtis was gone, his car easing down the street, and Albert was finally out of his hiding place.

"Did you hear what he said?" Margot asked when he joined her.

Albert dusted snow from his coat and trousers where he'd brushed against the hedge.

"I did."

"He might have been lying."

Albert had been thinking the same thing. "Did you notice that he was not in uniform?"

"Yes, he gets changed at work. Lots of us do. It's easier to keep it all there than have to cart it back and forth and Captain Allard expects everyone to look pristine when they start their shift."

Albert hoped she might put two and two together, but since she failed to draw the obvious conclusion, he helped her out.

"That means he needs to take his clothes off, Margot." Albert made the statement and waited to see if the penny dropped.

Margot blinked a couple of times, the cogs in her head churning until they aligned.

With a gasp of revulsion that made her take a pace back, she said, "No! No way. I'm not doing that."

Albert tilted his head. "All you need to do is get a look, Margot. He either has a bite mark or he does not. Knowing who attacked me last night won't tell us who killed Bjorn or who put that body in the ground, but it sure would be nice to solve one piece of this puzzle."

Chapter 29

Just as Margot claimed, the La Obrey police station was a two-minute walk from where Curtis lived. His car was in the parking lot, the roof and boot still covered in snow where he'd abandoned his attempt to remove it in favour of escaping Margot's questions.

Pausing outside, Margot gripped Albert's arm and steered him off the path.

"I need your phone number," she demanded. "We should have done this yesterday, but no matter, we can do it now.

Albert fished out his phone, holding it at the ready. He'd never been very good with his phone, once famously calling every contact in a group when he intended to message only one. That error worked in his favour at the time, but in a bid to learn the map function, the weather app, WhatsApp (whatever the heck that is), the camera and video function and a whole host of other applications he didn't even know existed, he'd taken lessons from his youngest granddaughter.

Apple-Blossom was, until his youngest son finally found a woman and produced children, the um, apple of his eye. More importantly, she grew up in an era when mobile phones, swiping left and right, searching the internet, and using voice commands to get information were second nature.

Confidently, Albert hit the 'contacts' symbol. A list of names appeared.

Squinting at the infernal device, he mumbled, "Oh, um."

"Shall I do it?" Margot held out her hand and with a sigh Albert handed his phone over thinking some remedial training might still be required.

Handing it back ten seconds later, Margot said, "There. My number is in your contacts, and I have yours. I will need you to create a distraction."

Albert's eyebrows aimed for his missing hairline. "Say what now?"

"A distraction, Albert. You want me to catch Curtis with his pants down and that means going into the male changing room. That's somewhere I have no plausible reason to be, so I want the option of a distraction when he goes in there, so I won't find myself surrounded by five naked men at the same time."

"Understood." Curious, even though it had been his idea, Albert asked, "How do you propose to catch a view of his back end?" His words were laced with an apologetic lilt.

Margot blew out an exasperated breath. "Well, a man and his pants are generally quite easy things to separate when a woman is involved."

His eyes flaring, Albert said, "You're not proposing to ..."

"Hell, no!" Margot shuddered. "The Allards are barely tolerable with their clothes on." Backing toward the station she added, "Just be ready with that distraction, okay, Albert? I want to be able to get out of there when the time comes."

She twisted to face the right way, turned left when she reached the station and vanished inside.

Albert watched her go, his mind tossing around ideas for ways he could divert the attention of the officers inside without getting himself arrested. Sending Rex to bite someone would do it, but would result in all manner of problems and the potential for Rex to be labelled as dangerous. Or he could feign a heart attack, but suddenly recovering when the ambulance arrived or Margot giving him the all-clear could still result in a trip to the local hospital. Plus the paramedics would know he was bluffing.

Inside the station, Margot waved at Marion Perrault behind the reception desk. Two years older, Marion was one of the few fellow officers she would label as a friend.

Surprised to see Margot, for she had heard the full report of the incident the previous evening, Marion called Margot over.

"What are you doing here? I thought you were suspended?"

Margot huffed. "I am. Hopefully Captain Allard will realise I was just trying to help, but I need to collect some things from my locker, and I was hoping to talk to Curtis. Is he in?"

"Curtis? Why do you want to talk to that sleazeball?"

Margot chuckled. "Because he is a sleazeball. I see the way he looks at my butt every chance he gets, so I want to use that to make him put in a good word for me with his dad."

Marion's scepticism was clear for anyone to see, but she said, "Okay, but don't say I didn't warn you. I don't think he's getting any at home, so if you suggest he might get lucky with you, I doubt you will ever hear the last of it."

Margot shrugged. "Gotta be worth a try."

Pushing through the door when Marion buzzed her in, Margot went to the locker rooms. Glancing left and right to make sure she was not being watched, a spike of fear shot through her when she saw Curtis coming. He was still limping heavily, but joking about something with his brother Richard.

Pushing against the leftmost door to enter the men's locker room instead of the women's to the right, she peered cautiously around and listened. There was no sound coming from within.

Whispering words her mother would not approve of, yet which seemed wholly appropriate for her current situation, Margot closed the door and waited for Curtis to arrive. He would be startled to see her again so soon. Even more so that she was in the male changing area, but how should she approach her task?

She needed to see his bottom. He was going on shift, not coming off, so the likelihood that he might take a shower was slim. She could act sexy and convince him to take off his pants; that would be easy enough, but what then?

Pulling a grimace at the prospect, Margot ran through a dozen scenarios before spotting the open locker. There were more lockers than officers, so it stood to reason that there would be empty ones.

The voices of Curtis and his brother were now right outside the door. It opened a few inches, Curtis starting to come through before stopping to finish listening to what his brother had to say.

Bolting for the locker, Margot questioned if she would fit despite her petite frame, but she did, sliding in sideways and pulling the door to. Leaving it open an inch, she had an angle through which she could see one side of the locker room.

Breathing as quietly as she could, she settled in to wait.

Outside in the cold December air, Albert continued to rack his brains. Every idea he came up with he quickly dismissed because it would draw too much attention or result in injury to himself, Rex, or someone else.

He thought about borrowing a bike which he would then crash in the snow right outside the station's glass windows. The people inside would come to his aid and that would create the distraction Margot wanted. Albert was convinced he would break his hip though because Rex would knock him off thinking it to be a game.

He also considered starting a fire because that would evacuate all the personnel from the station. On the face of it, a fire was a great option, but the station would have CCTV coverage around the premises and once they reviewed it, he could guarantee himself a spell in a cell.

Becoming frustrated with himself, he asked Rex.

"We need a distraction, dog. Got any suggestions?"

Rex was only half listening. His bits were getting cold, and he wanted to be moving. Addressed by his human, he came from sitting to standing, wagging his tail.

Albert ruffled his fur. "Doing okay, Rex?"

"Well my testicles have shrunk to the size of peanuts in this cold, but otherwise I'm doing fine. What's going on?"

Albert heard Rex's strange sounds and wondered, as always, what they might mean.

To kill time, he picked up some snow and an idea formed. "I know, how about a game of fetch?"

Inside the men's locker room, Margot peeked out from her hiding place. Curtis was singing to himself, an offkey rendition of a Shania Twain song. Margot wanted him to just get on with the task of getting undressed, but he appeared to be in no hurry whatsoever.

Nevertheless, as her legs started to cramp from holding her awkward position, Curtis stripped off his shirt. It went on a hanger and his uniform shirt came out. First he donned a thin cotton t-shirt, over which he placed the regulation stab vest. On top of those he would wear his shirt and then the thick winter coat that came with their uniform.

It was hard to see what he was doing; her angle was wrong, but until he got to his bottom half, she didn't need to care.

He sat to undo the laces on his thick winter boots and kicked them off, giving Margot a first look at his feet and ankles. She had to strain her eyes to see, but she could not discern that one was bigger than the other.

He stood once more, unbuckling his belt and dropping his trousers. Margot got to watch when he scratched his backside and rearranged the items at the front, and had to pray he couldn't hear the thoughts in her head.

All she needed was for the idiot to turn one way or the other. If he turned around she would get a good look at his butt and that was all she needed. When he stepped out of his trousers and folded them neatly, she was able to confirm there was no sign of swelling around either of his ankles. It wasn't definitive, but his claim to have twisted his ankle looked less and less true by the second.

Taking out his uniform trousers and lowering them to step in, he finally twisted to face away from her, but in so doing, he lost balance and in correcting himself moved out of her range of vision. She needed to move to be able to see.

Leaning out of the locker, she tried to see his butt. Was there a dressing evident beneath the thin cotton of his underwear? He was pulling his trousers up – she had a second at most before she would miss her chance and have to resort to something more drastic, but she couldn't lean out far enough to see him without altering her grip.

Outside in the cold, Albert threw snowballs for Rex. It wasn't something he'd ever done before but that was because it hardly ever snowed in their home village in the southeast of England. Rex evidently loved the game, leaping to catch them as Albert imagined he would. Each time he caught one, he would chomp it to pieces and spit out the icy cold mess it made. Then he would prance excitedly on his paws in anticipation of the next one.

Albert was waiting for Margot to call or message to tell him to spring the trap, and was testing his aim to see how close he could get to the police station doors. His plan was to 'accidentally' launch one just a little farther than he had been. The doors were automatic, so if he threw a snowball and Rex chased it, Albert believed he could trigger the doors and have his dog end up inside.

It wasn't much as distractions went, but it was all he'd been able to come up with.

However, the doors opened unexpectedly, two officers on their way out suddenly faced with a snowball and an onrushing German Shepherd whose attention was singularly focused on the white sphere arcing through the air.

Albert, his face pulled into a grimace of grim anticipation, managed to shout, "Rex, nooooo!" But he did not do so in time to stop his dog leaping into the air to intercept the snowball.

Unaware of the events unfolding outside, Margot's jaw was beginning to ache from how hard she had it clenched. However, in leaning out just that little bit further to get a view of Curtis's back end, her fingers slipped and she spilled, swearing with shock as she fell from the locker to sprawl on the floor six feet from her target.

Startled, Curtis shot through a one hundred and eighty degree turn to land facing the woman on the floor. His trousers were up, but still undone.

Wishing the floor would swallow her and praying hard that she could achieve invisibility in the next half second, Margot looked up from her prone position.

"Um, hi?" she tried.

A lecherous grin spread across Curtis's face. "Hello indeed. Spying on old Curtis, were you? Well, there's no need to be shy, Margot. I've got just what you want right here." He dropped his trousers again.

Margot threw up in her mouth a little, muttering, "Ewww."

Curtis kicked off his trousers and came forward, palm out and flat to suggest she should stay where she was.

"No need to get up," he cooed, his voice filled with husky, dark tones. "I've got something you can do while you are down there."

Scrambling backward to get away, Margot hit the lockers to her rear and had to jump to her feet. Curtis continued to advance though and whatever thoughts were going through his head were altering the shape of things in his pants.

Opening her mouth, and having no idea what might come out of it, Margot was saved by a commotion outside.

Chapter 30

Rex flew through the air, his eyes locked on the snowball and nothing else. Consequently, when he barrelled into the chest of the female officer on her way out of the station, it startled him.

Taking his eyes off the snowball, he missed it, but crashing to the ground on top of the woman, he caught sight of it slamming into the face of her partner.

Albert had both hands covering his face. Peering through his fingers, he gave momentary thought to simply legging it. Rex would catch up when he called, but while the tactic might work in a city where he could vanish into the crowd, here they would simply track him to Celeste's guesthouse.

The female officer, a woman in her early forties called Eloise, with five kids and a stay-at-home layabout husband, wheezed and struggled to draw a breath. Rex had knocked the air from her lungs when they hit the ground with him on top and now they were lying half in half out of the station with the automatic doors trying to slide shut.

Marion and everyone else inside ran to her aid, with the exception of her partner, Remy, who didn't like her all that much and was too busy glaring at the old man who threw the snowball to care if she was hurt.

Albert rushed over. "Goodness, I'm so sorry. I was just exercising my dog. Is everyone okay?"

Rex wagged his tail and licked the downed woman's face. "*I'm fine,*" he slobbered. "*How are you?*"

Eloise slapped and fought against Rex's wet tongue, protesting, "Get off! Get off!" until she discovered that opening her mouth gave the dog a chance to slip his tongue into it. After that she kept it firmly closed and considered drawing her sidearm.

Elsewhere in the station, Margot used the distraction to slip around Curtis. She still hadn't got a look at his backside but had noticed one thing.

"What happened to your limp?" she accused, backing toward the door and making sure to keep a safe distance between them.

Curtis looked down at his feet as though confused before sniggering at his mistake. "Ah, you got me. I don't have a limp. I didn't twist my ankle. I just didn't fancy spending the night at Drucker's Field. Nevermind that though, what about us?" He patted his groin. "I've still got something here for you."

Shuddering again, Margot's stomach churned like someone had just offered her a bowl of cold cat sick to eat. Running from the locker room, she found a glut of her colleagues in reception all staring at Eloise lying on the ground where she was receiving mouth to mouth from Albert's dog.

Arriving behind everyone with them all looking at the old man outside, she waved to get Albert's attention, indicated that she was going to go around, and headed for the station's side door that led to the carpark.

They rendezvoused two minutes later after Albert managed to haul Rex away from his latest game and got through a thousand apologies.

The cops eyed him suspiciously, but doubting they could prove the snowball was thrown with malicious intent, they let him go.

"Well?" he asked.

"He was faking the limp," Margot explained. "He's not the one who attacked you."

Albert huffed out a breath of disappointment. It occurred to him to ask how she got to check Curtis's backside, but decorum dictated he keep the question to himself.

"So, what's next?" she asked, checking her watch. "I'm afraid you have missed the library and council offices; they will be closed for lunch now."

Albert pulled a face; he really wanted to know who it was that opposed the archaeological dig. If he was right, it could prove to be the smoking gun that would lead them to a killer responsible for two murders many years apart.

"When will it reopen?" He fervently hoped she wouldn't say, 'Tomorrow'.

"At two o'clock, but that's assuming they open on time. The place is run by volunteers, and they can be a bit iffy with their hours. It will reopen though. We just have to hope it isn't Simone and Valerie working there today."

"Why's that?"

Margot huffed out a breath. "Because they are odious, petty women and Valerie hates me."

Albert almost asked why, but his brain was wise enough to stomp hard on the question before it left his mouth. Thankfully, Margot suggested an alternative activity.

"You said you wanted to visit the morgue so you could speak to the coroner about the body."

"That's right," Albert nodded grimly. "Now you might not like the next part of the plan."

Chapter 31

Like it Margot did not. Back in uniform, she knew without question that she now ran the risk of losing her job. Albert convinced her it was necessary if they hoped to learn anything. The coroner's office and the morgue were in Brubourg, the next town along from La Obrey where she would not be known. Only by arriving in uniform would she be able to ask questions and reasonably expect to get answers.

Even so, it was still a risky proposition and Margot grumbled all the way there.

"What if someone does recognise me? What if captain Allard or anyone else is there to ask questions about the body? They must be waiting for answers too."

"No," Albert replied, his eyes on the mountains, "I don't think Captain Allard is looking for information about the body Rex found. I think he knows precisely who it is."

"You really believe he could be involved?" Margot saw no need to hide her doubt. Sure, her boss was acting odd and the whole thing with Bjorn Ironfoundersson needed some explanation, but she wasn't ready to see him as a killer.

"Involved? Yes, but I'm not sure at what level. Being involved in the cover up doesn't make him the killer. We will know more once we have spoken to the coroner." He left it at that, his thoughts his own while Margot drove through Brubourg on the town's main road.

Rex snoozed on the backseat, questioning, as he so often did, why the humans didn't ask him to track down the killer. The village was small enough that he could probably walk a circuit and find where the man lived. He wasn't claiming to have worked out all the pieces of the case, but the same person followed the first victim and attacked his human. That made him guilty of one crime at the very least.

The coroner's building sat at the edge of town in a municipal district with other services and next to a fire station. Margot had been there only once before on her second day on the job. Sent to collect the personal effects of a tourist who suffered a heart attack and died during his dinner at one of La Obrey's restaurants, she had never been farther than the reception desk.

She didn't want to reveal or even admit to herself how nervous she felt walking into the vaguely familiar building. It would have been bad enough if she was there on genuine police business, but knowing she was about to spew lie after lie in a bid to get to the bottom of the mystery surrounding Drucker's Field and the body buried in it, she felt positively sick.

Rex got left in the car, but it was warm on the backseat, and he settled in to get some sleep.

Margot flashed a smile at the man behind the reception desk. She guessed his age to be somewhere around thirty and thought he looked vaguely familiar, though she couldn't place him.

Looking up, the man opened his mouth and shut it again.

"Hello. I'm Officer Dubois …"

"Margot?"

Margot's next words died in her mouth.

"Little Margot. Goodness, you sure grew up."

Narrowing her eyes a little, she asked, "Do I know you?" There was no way to miss the warning tone in her voice.

The man chuckled. "I remember the fieriness too." Able to see Margot was about to get annoyed, he quickly added, "I'm Daniel Seigner. I used to date your sister about fifteen years ago."

Margot's cheeks flushed, recalling the boy she could now recognise in the man before her. She'd had such a crush on him at the time.

"Danny," she said, her cheeks still burning. "I didn't recognise you. Hold on," she frowned, "I thought you went to medical school. Isn't that why you dumped my sister?"

Danny chuckled. "That's not quite how I remember things, but yes, I went to medical school."

"So why are you working on the reception desk in a morgue?"

A door to their right opened, a pregnant woman in her thirties coming through it. She was pale and looked awful. "Sorry about that, Dr Seigner. This morning sickness is kicking my butt."

"That's perfectly all right, Brigitte. Just buzz me if you feel sick again. And if you need to go home, you only have to say. I can find cover for you."

Brigitte flopped down into the chair which Dr Seigner now held. "Not a chance. This baby has taken enough already and it's not even here yet. I'm going to keep working until the last minute, thank you."

Daniel held the chair steady until Brigitte was settled then turned his attention to Margot and Albert.

"Shall we?"

He was already walking to the door Brigitte came through. It bore the legend 'Staff Only' in bold letters at eye height and was the only door in the reception area unless one wanted to go back outside.

Going through it, he said over his shoulder, "I assume you are here about the mystery man they found last night."

Margot expected to have to prove who she was and jump through hoops to get to speak to anyone, let alone the coroner. Discovering she knew the man who held the answers was beyond what she could have hoped for, and she wasn't about to look a gift horse in the mouth.

Hurrying after Daniel, she asked, "How long have you been the coroner here?"

"Oh, I'm not the coroner. I'm her assistant. She's currently performing an autopsy, but will have to stop soon to meet with your boss. I figure that's why you are here." He was leading them down a corridor wide enough to allow wheeled gurneys to transport bodies in and out of the building. Pausing with his hand on a door marked 'Assistant Coroner', he continued, "To make sure everything is set up before his arrival, yes?"

Margot nodded vigorously, lying through her teeth while her stomach performed back flips.

"Yes. Yes, that's right. Captain Allard likes to have things ready for him."

Daniel pushed the door open, holding it so Margot and then Albert could follow. When Albert drew near, he held out his right hand.

"Daniel Siegner."

Albert met his firm grip with one of his own. "Albert Smith."

"Ah, yes. I thought I recognised you. You are helping the police with their enquiries?"

Margot flared her eyes, warning Albert to be careful what answer he gave. If Captain Allard was expected soon, they had a small window to get some answers and leave, but they also needed to somehow convince Daniel to conveniently forget to mention they had ever been there.

"Something like that," Albert chose his words carefully. Hoping to alter the topic of conversation, he asked, "What can you tell us about the body found last night?" Albert could tell the doctor was savvy enough to know they were avoiding his questions. Margot failed to sound convincing when she lied about the reason for their visit and Albert had simply changed the subject.

However, Dr Seigner accepted it and moved to a desk where a wide monitor screen sat above a keyboard.

Tapping a few keys, he brought up a file.

"The subject is male, aged between twenty-five and thirty-five. It's not possible to be more exact with the level of decomposition. However, it is possible to estimate how long the body has been in the ground with a little more confidence. In all likelihood, he was buried in the early seventies, roughly fifty years ago."

Albert absorbed the news. It changed things. His assumption thus far was that Captain Allard had some involvement. Perhaps not as the killer, but a police officer who, for whatever reason, saw fit to help cover up the death. But Captain Allard was in his early fifties and the likely date of death ruled him out.

"How sure are you?" Albert pressed the assistant coroner.

"Of the date he was buried? Fairly certain. The state of decomposition combined with the growth of ..."

Albert waved for him to stop. He already knew enough about what happened to a body once it went in the ground. He didn't need to be put off his food for the next week with gory details.

"What else can you tell us?"

"He was murdered." Dr Seigner delivered the shocking, yet unsurprising, statement and waited for their reaction. When it was clear this was what they expected to hear he added, "A single stab wound to the chest that penetrated his heart. It entered his ribcage at an upward angle suggesting a shorter person delivered the wound. Otherwise, though it is difficult to be sure about superficial wounds to his flesh – since it is no longer there – there appear to be no other wounds."

It was as Albert expected. People do not find themselves in shallow graves by accident. The man was murdered and the crime hidden from the people of La Obrey by those who conspired to keep it a secret.

Dr Seigner continued to talk, explaining that the victim was a muscular man standing six feet and two inches tall. That would have made him a giant fifty years ago and lengthened the list of suspects since almost everyone would be shorter.

His clothes had dobs of paint on them; Dr Seigner showed them photographs. Albert's first thought was that the victim was a decorator, but the blobs of paint were in a multitude of colours and Dr Seigner had been thorough in his investigation.

"It's oil paint," he revealed. "The kind an artist uses. That doesn't mean he painted full time, but he was wearing the shirt when he was stabbed," a new photograph showed the hole in the shirt, "so I believe this was a hobby at least."

They were building a picture of the victim, but the one thing they needed more than anything was a name.

"Sorry," Dr Seigner puffed out his cheeks. "There was no identification on him. No wallet, no tattoos, no marking of any kind. I have been able to use a 3D render of his skull to compose an image of his face. These tools are getting more sophisticated all the time and their accuracy is surprising. However, any scarring would not show up, so if his face was disfigured, we would not be able to see it here."

He clicked with the mouse, selecting a different tab and a face appeared on the screen. The head was bald and Dr Seigner explained that the ears and nose could be wrong, but Albert and Margot were looking at the face of the man in the ground. A man who was murdered fifty years ago and whose secrets yearned to be told.

Then Dr Seigner said something Albert hadn't expected.

Chapter 32

"He's American?" Margot questioned. "How can you tell?"

"The dentistry." Dr Seigner clicked the mouse again, taking them to a 3D picture of the victim's teeth. "Ideally we would be able to identify his remains from his teeth, but records do not go back that far. However, the crowns on three of his back molars contain dental amalgam. Its use was common practice for many years, but the American Dental Association specified a mix of tin, copper, zinc, and silver at very specific percentages. His match those percentages, and because most of his fillings were performed when he was a teenager – he was overdue to have most of them replaced – he is most likely an American."

They had a nameless American man who was stabbed to death fifty years ago and buried in a shallow grave. The single stab wound told them the attack was not frenzied, but there was little else to learn.

The door to their room opened inward without warning which caused Margot to spasm in panic. However, a female figure filled the doorway, an attractive brunette woman in her forties. She was still putting a white coat over the top of her clothes and fighting a little with the collar.

"Dr Seigner," she nodded at Margot and Albert.

Daniel replied, "Dr Duvauchelle. Have you finished with your autopsy?"

"No, but Brigitte paged me to say the police from La Obrey are here." Her eyebrows ruffled, her face quizzical as she took in Margot's uniform. "But I see you already knew that. Can you handle them?"

"Of course. Please leave it with me."

Dr Duvauchelle withdrew, turning left to go away from the reception as she returned to her work. Margot was looking at Albert until she felt Daniel's eyes upon her. When she looked his way he folded his arms.

"Would you like to tell me why you're so jumpy about your boss arriving?"

"No, not really," Margot murmured.

"Look, I'm not a fool, Margot. "Clearly you want to keep your activities secret and I guess I don't need to know the reasons behind it. Perhaps you would like me to omit to mention that you were here."

Speaking for her, Albert said, "That would be very much appreciated, Dr Seigner."

"I suppose you would also like to leave by the back door?"

Margot nodded. "Very much so. The situation is a little hard to explain."

"Then perhaps you should not even attempt to do so. If I know nothing, I can reveal nothing. Although …" He left the final word hanging in the air for a few seconds before adding, "perhaps you might like to explain things more fully over dinner next week."

His forwardness caught Margot off guard, her cheeks flushing, but she managed to mumble, "Um, sure. That sounds lovely."

They stood looking at each other for a few seconds before Albert felt a need to interject. Thinking there was too little time to be wasting it on flirting, he said, "Give him your number, Margot, and be quick about it." Then, aiming his attention at the assistant coroner, he prompted, "You said something about a back door?"

Leaving the assistant coroner's office they could hear voices echoing through from the reception area. Through the frosted glass window, they could see the indistinct shapes of the police officers on the other side. Hustling down the corridor, they followed Daniel until they reached a set of double doors that exited into the car park.

Albert shook the man's hand as did Margot. Her car was parked just a short distance away, but so were two of La Obrey's squad cars. Was there anyone waiting in them? They could not see from their current position and would have to run the gauntlet if they wanted to escape.

Ducking low, Margot made a run for her car, and reaching it angled her eyes to see if there was anybody waiting in one of the squad cars. Confident they were empty, she waved for Albert to join her and breathing a sigh of relief slipped into the driver's seat.

Rex had been enjoying a dream involving three lady dogs and discarded pizza, but awoke the moment Margot touched her door handle to get in. Now sitting up with his jowls on sideways from where he'd been sleeping, he questioned how much time had passed.

Albert gave his dog a pat on the head and instructed him to stay where he was because they were leaving. They were armed with new information. How much of it would prove useful only time would determine, but Albert felt that they had moved a step closer to figuring out just what was going on in the tiny French village.

What he did not see as they pulled away was the face looking out through the assistant coroner's office window. Had he done so, Albert would have known just how much trouble they were now in.

Chapter 33

They were both quiet in the car on the way back to La Obrey, each thinking feverish thoughts about the new developments and what logical step they could take next.

Breaking the silence, Margot said, "Captain Allard cannot have had anything to do with this." She was stating the obvious and went on to say, "He would have been a little boy when the American artist was killed."

Albert watched the landscape going by outside his window. "That is undeniable, yet he appears to be involved anyway."

"Is he?" Margot challenged. "I don't see how he can be."

Taking off his cap and scratching at an itch on his skull, Albert grumpily admitted, "Neither do I. But why else would he be acting the way he is?"

Arriving in La Obrey, Albert sought to confirm, "We're going to the library, right?" He checked his watch. "It will have reopened by now."

"Yes, but I need to go home first. It's one thing to put my uniform on to go to Brubourg, and another entirely to walk around in my home village where everyone knows that I have been suspended from work."

Albert chose not to argue. Rex had been in the car for some time after all and a walk would do him good. Coming from Margot's house also meant they would pass his guest house which gave him the opportunity to quiz Celeste about her memories of American artists in the village fifty years ago.

Rex was snoozing on the back seat until they pulled to a stop and he heard Margot apply her hand brake. He was ready to get out of the car, having been cooped up in it for the best part of two hours now. Clambering out and onto the snow-clad pavement, he pushed his front legs out far in front of his body to perform a complicated stretch that involved all his limbs independently.

Margot excused herself to run into her house to change, leaving Albert and Rex in the street.

"*Did you discover anything of interest at the coroners?*" asked Rex.

Hearing his dog's odd noises, Albert looked down at him.

"What was that, old boy? Asking about food, were you?"

Rex might have rolled his eyes had he been a human, or perhaps given a sad shake of his head. As neither of those expressions meant anything to a dog he barked instead.

"*Why don't you ever listen to me? Why do I have to explain everything three times and speak as slowly as possible? I smelled the body almost a day before you took me back to the field to show you it. And I've been smelling the person who attacked you all over this village. If you just let me off the lead and try to keep up, I reckon I could find his house.*"

Startled by his dog's sudden ferocious barking, Albert looked around to see who else had heard. Thankfully it was the middle of the day and not late at night when Rex's barking might wake a child. But whatever message Rex was trying to convey, Albert believed it could be done with less volume.

Coming down into a crouch with one knee in the snow, Albert stroked the side of Rex's face.

"I wish I understood you better than I do." It was a heartfelt sentiment born of the belief that his dog genuinely had something interesting to say.

Rex licked his human's chin. Telling himself to be calm and patient, he said, "sorry, I know you are doing the best you can. I guess I'll have to find another way to show you."

Margot's front door opened, closing again a moment later with her outside. She locked it and edged her way carefully down her sloping drive to join her companions in the street.

"To the library then?" she confirmed.

Setting off with Rex leading, Albert said, "Yes, via my guest house. I should like to ask Celeste another question." He felt a little bad about constantly pestering his landlady, but the simple truth of it was that she had been very forthcoming with information so far, seemed thoroughly knowledgeable about village affairs, and was one of the oldest residents, so her memory would go back further than most.

Rex happily sniffed his way back to the guest house, dismissing the now faint scent of his human's attacker. He believed it was the leftover smell from this morning when he traced it to the disappointing find of the handkerchief beneath the snow. However, the moment Albert opened the front door of the guest house, Rex's powerful nose supplied him with a fresh burst of the same odour.

Albert was trying to stamp the snow from his boots before stepping over the threshold, and nearly lost his right arm when Rex surged forward into the property.

"Whoa there, boy! Where are you going in such a hurry? Can you smell food by any chance?"

"*Are you kidding me?*" barked Rex. "*He's here!*"

Albert was having to lean back and use his left arm against the door frame to keep Rex from dragging him into the building. But fighting to get him under control was proving impossible, so before the mad German shepherd yanked him off his feet, Albert chose to let go.

"What's got into him?" asked Margot.

Undoing his laces with hurried fingers, Albert kicked off his boots and chased after his dog, calling over his shoulder, "I've no idea but it's probably going to result in trouble."

Rex ran through the guest house, his nose working overtime to track the scent, but it was everywhere. The man who attacked his human had been here recently and for all Rex knew he was yet to leave.

He could hear his human calling for him, shouting his name and demanding he return, but that was because the old man didn't know what Rex knew. It was his job to protect Albert from himself when it was necessary and that included occasions such as right now.

Using his head to barge through doors, Rex searched as much of the ground floor of the house as he could reach. The man he wanted had been here recently, his particular odour permeated the air in many of the rooms he visited, but he did not appear to be here now. Rex checked the stairs just to confirm his target had not ascended them, but having exhausted the hiding places in the house, he paused to think.

Albert raced directly to the kitchen where he expected to once again find his dog helping himself to food. Surprised yet grateful to find the room devoid of canine mayhem, he set about looking elsewhere. He found him at the foot of the stairs where his dog sat calmly as though contemplating something complicated.

Quashing his urge to berate his dog for running off, Albert instead asked him what had spurred his mad dash through the guesthouse.

Pleased by the question, for it showed great insight for a human, Rex did his best to explain. However, the communication barrier between human and dog proved as insurmountable on this occasion as it almost always did.

Accepting defeat and thankful Rex had not wrought further destruction upon Celeste's guesthouse, Albert called out for her. He did not, however, expect an answer. He'd been shouting Rex's name for the last minute and were she in the house, Albert felt certain she would have come to see what was causing the commotion.

"She's outside," advised Margot. Pointing to a figure beyond the nearest window. She had her boots in her hand having doffed them before entering much like Albert.

Celeste was indeed outside where she was wrestling something out of a garden shed.

Albert and Margot trudged back to the front door, stopped to put their boots back on, and made their way around the side of the house to find Celeste. Rex's lead was clamped tightly in Albert's right hand, half of the leather wrapped around his gloved mitt to keep the dog close.

"*Ask her about the man that was just in her house,*" Rex encouraged.

Of course, Albert didn't do that. He focused instead on the question he came to ask. First though he offered to help with whatever Celeste was doing.

"Oh I'm just fighting my way back to where I keep a couple of old wooden sledges. During the winter season I get quite a few families staying and the children like to do a bit of tobogganing. There are some good slopes here for it. I remember a bit of tobogganing myself when I was a girl."

"I can help with that," volunteered Margot, forging her way into the shed and leaving Albert to pose his question.

"An American artist?" Celeste appeared confused by the question. "In La Obrey?"

"Yes," confirmed Albert. "You will recall I asked you about people who vanished. Well in all likelihood the body they found in the field was buried there fifty years ago and it is entirely possible he was an artist from America."

Celeste shrugged her shoulders, shook her head, and offered Albert a hopeless expression.

"I'm sorry Albert, but I don't recall anyone ever going missing. I've been thinking hard about it ever since you asked me last night. I even asked some of my friends, the older persons within the village, and they all said the same. I can ask if anyone recalls there ever being an artist staying here, but I doubt very much that anyone will. Could it be that the coroner is wrong and the body is much older than that?"

Albert made a face as he wrestled with how to answer but in the end all he could say was, "No, I don't think so. In my experience a coroner will give no information at all unless they are quite certain that what they're saying is accurate. Approximately fifty years ago a man was murdered in this town and his body has been lying unnoticed in a shallow grave less than half a mile from your house ever since."

Extricating the sledges proved to be a more demanding task than she had anticipated, but in many ways it made Margot glad that she had volunteered. Otherwise the octogenarian guesthouse owner would still be trying to do it. Carrying it above her head, she clambered over some empty crates of beer and a few garden tools before depositing it on the ground by Celeste's feet.

Pointing with an apologetic finger, Celeste said, "I'm sorry, there's a second one back there if you can find it."

Two minutes later, Albert and Margot had carried the sledges to the front of Celeste's guest house where they were now stacked against one of the outside walls. Yet again, Albert's landlady had been forthcoming with information, but ultimately of no assistance whatsoever.

Their attempts to interrogate the information they hoped to find at the library had been thwarted twice already, but setting off through the village once again they were determined that this time they would find who it was in the village who opposed the Swedish application for their archaeological dig.

"Imagine how quickly we could get there if we took the toboggans," Margot joked, a smile lighting up her face.

Albert sniggered at the suggestion. "But would we stop when we got there?" he questioned. It was a straight downhill shot from Celeste's place at the top of the village. A long road with a slow curve ran through the houses to the main road that bisected La Obrey. The library, more houses, several businesses, and the park lay beyond it. Attempting to sled from point A to point B would be suicide, the happy tobogganer picking up speed almost the whole way until they would stop suddenly upon hitting a wall.

They joked about it a little as they walked, Margot regaling her older companion with a story about how she'd 'borrowed' her mum's best silver tray when her own sled broke and how it ended up rather worse off for the adventure.

Watching them walk down the hill away from her guest house Celeste Darroze picked up her house phone. The hand holding it shook so badly that she needed the other just to hold it steady against her ear. Biting down against her rising panic, she dialled a number she was coming to know by heart.

Chapter 34

Lars fought his frustration. There was precious little of the field left to survey and his back was getting sore from the awkward motion of using the metal detector. In the last few hours he'd managed to find four ring pulls, three rusty cans, an old spanner, a weight plate from somebody's barbell, multiple nails and screws, and not one single haul of plundered Nazi gold.

He was refusing to give up, but even in doing so he questioned his own sanity. All the evidence suggested that he was searching in the wrong location. Stopping so he could put the metal detector down and stretch off his aching back, he looked around at the surrounding countryside. Everything was pristine white, except for where he had walked, and where the police and forensic teams had traipsed back and forth in their task of exhuming and removing the body.

Could it be the map was incorrectly marked? Eighty years had elapsed since Walter Karlsson buried his treasure, a period long enough that trees may have been felled and new ones planted. Fence lines could have moved and the map he was working from was hardly the best he'd ever seen.

So if it wasn't in this field? Where was it? Peter and Julienne had already departed, leaving him as the sole archaeologist in the village. People had already been asking questions and growing suspicious about their activities. That old English man especially. The longer Lars stayed in La Obrey, the more likely it was that his lies would be exposed.

Believing he had a limited window within which to find that which he came for, he pulled out the map once more. Using his phone to bring up Google Earth, he compared one with the other and questioned why he had not done so before. Instantly, he saw that the tree line in the 1940s was 30 or more feet back from where it sat today. On the copy they were given of Walter Karlsson's map, the plundered gold was buried just beyond the tree line a yard or so into the field.

That was where they had expected to find it, and it was only when they failed to do so that their search parameters expanded.

Now he realised they had always been searching in the wrong place. The gold had to be inside the tree line, and not very far from where the white forensic tent now sat.

Biting his lip, Lars told himself that he had no choice other than to proceed with the crazy plan in his head. The lone cop now guarding the tent until the forensics people decided they had found all there was to find, would watch his activities out of boredom, but he would not question them.

When the metallic whine echoed shrilly in his ears less than five minutes after starting his search between the trees, Lars knew that he had found Walter Karlsson's stash of gold and had to fight not to display his excitement in view of the young police officer.

Surreptitiously checking to see if the young man had even noticed, Lars continued to waft the metal detector over the area. When he found small items, such as cans or the spanner, the whining noise claiming there to be something metallic beneath the ground faded almost immediately. Now it was a steady, constant, insistent squeal that filled his ears and demanded he turn down the volume. Whatever was under the soil, it was big.

Checking the map once more and trying to keep a lid on his rising exhilaration, Lars convinced himself that this was it. He continued to survey the area for a further thirty minutes, making sure there were no other signals to be found, but really he was just putting off what he knew he needed to do next.

There was no way to excavate whatever was beneath the surface in full view of anyone, let alone a police officer. Were he to even start digging, the young man would surely come to investigate.

Lars had already acknowledged the need for a diversion and could think of only one thing that would demand a police officer abandoned their post: a colleague in trouble.

Chapter 35

Captain Allard clenched his fist. He had genuinely believed, had allowed himself to be convinced, that the situation could be managed without the need for escalation or violence. That was clearly no longer the case.

He could not involve his sons or anyone else under his command. The family secret had to die with him. Not that they would be desperately horrified or shocked by what he had to reveal, but he had carried the burden of truth for more than a decade and would fight tooth and nail to spare his children the same misery.

His call with Celeste was the final nail in the coffin, showing him that no matter how hard he tried to plug the gaps, the truth was getting closer and closer to leaking out. The old man continued to ask questions and his most junior member of staff aided Albert Smith's attempts to expose that which would benefit everyone to remain hidden.

Celeste did not want anyone to get hurt, but her request was childish. They were already beyond that stage and of all the people involved in the conspiracy she was the one who ought to see the need for Margot Dubois and Albert Smith to be silenced.

Until two days ago, if one ignored the secret he carried, Captain Allard had upheld the laws of his nation with due diligence since the first day he put on his uniform. Whether he would put it on again tomorrow and feel comfortable in it he could not tell, but his course of action was already determined, and he could see no way to avoid it.

The truth had to remain hidden.

Chapter 36

Arriving at the library to find it was, in fact, open, Margot said, "Hi, Claudette," to the woman behind the desk, who looked up briefly as they passed. Had she looked a little closer, she might have noticed the rather large German shepherd Albert was sneaking in with him.

There had been a conversation about not 'watering' the books or shelves they would find inside, though Albert was fairly confident Rex's bladder had to be more or less empty after all the lampposts and fences he marked coming through the village. It was too cold to leave him chained to a fence outside, so Albert was bringing him in regardless of what anyone had to say on the subject.

Passing a duo of desks arranged against one wall with a pair of ageing computers mounted on them, Margot stopped.

"This is a research resource," she remarked, poking at a mouse to see if the screen would come to life. "We might find out more about the American artist there. I haven't used it before, well not since a school project more than a decade ago, but I remember that it holds the repository of images and newspaper clippings from the local paper. That goes back about a century."

"That might be a good idea," agreed Albert. "Let's see what the paperwork trail will tell us about the architects dig site and who opposed it first though, eh?"

Margot moved on. The library area itself could not be described as big or extensively stocked. In fact, Albert thought perhaps he knew people with more books in their houses. Nevertheless there were sections broken down by genre and by age group and even a small large-print section if he was reading the labels in French correctly.

At the back of the room in a corner, a door marked 'Town Hall' led into a small open space.

"We go in through a different door when there's a meeting," Margot explained. "But any other time the only way in is through the library."

There were stacks of chairs against one wall, ready to be spread out and arranged when there was need. To their left as they entered, two ladies were hunched over a table arguing about something.

Margot sighed and grimaced. "That's Simone Roussel and her daughter Valerie. The last people we wanted to be here today."

They were too engrossed in what they were doing to notice there was someone new in the room until Margot cleared her throat. They were crossing the floor, Rex's claws clicking on the hard surface.

Both women looked up. The older of the two, Simone, had lustrous blonde locks. Albert judged her age to be somewhere in her mid-fifties though she looked distinctly younger and he only arrived at that conclusion due to the apparent age of her daughter. Valerie wore her hair in a functional, if somewhat less attractive, page boy cut and looked very little like her mother.

"Margot? What brings you here today?" asked Simone.

"Well, it won't be police business," sniped Valerie in a manner that made Albert think there was some bad blood between the two women.

Margot offered Valerie a tight smile. "No, that's correct, Valerie. I am not here on police business." Turning her eyes towards the elder of the Roussel women, she went on to say, "I would like to see the application to dig on Drucker's Field, please."

Simone's eyebrows raised in response to the request and her mouth shifted in a way that made Albert believe she might refuse or ask for an explanation why. She did neither, choosing instead to opt for the favoured bureaucratic response of, "You'll need to fill in a form."

With a small sigh, Margot withdrew a pen from a coat pocket and with a click to extend the nib asked, "Which form, please?"

Valerie crossed the room to a filing cabinet behind a counter and returned a moment later with a form on pink paper.

"There is a fee too," she advised, sounding pleased to be able to announce the news.

Her voice dripping with honey, Margot took the form, said, "Thank you so much," and made her way back to the door to leave the village hall.

Confused about where she was going, and caught out by her sudden departure, Albert found himself stranded in front of the two ladies, his feet twitching with indecision. Was he expected to follow Margot? Or wait here for her momentary return?

"Come along, Albert," she called as she reached the door, holding it open until he caught up with her. "This won't take a moment." Dropping her voice to a whisper, she added, "But the less time I spend in that foul woman's presence the better. Plus, we can use the time to do some research."

The form was all in French, obviously, but had it been in English Albert suspected he would still have struggled; official forms were just like that - deliberately confusing to the inexperienced form filler.

Margot settled into one of the two chairs facing the pair of computers at the research station. Clicking the mouse she bought hers to life, then leaned across and did the same for the one at the empty station.

Feeling he was being prompted to do so, Albert slipped into the seat. However, the login, the password, and everything that came after it, was also in French.

"Sorry," Albert interrupted Margot's scribbling, "My French just isn't up to this task."

Pushing the form to one side, Margot leaned across to Albert's desk, twisted the keyboard so it was angled towards her, and typed in the password which was written above the monitor.

With a swoop of the mouse and a few clicks, she brought up a translation tool.

"You can just type your search parameters in here in English and it will translate them. Then you can copy and paste them into the search bar." She pointed to where Albert needed to look.

Puffing out his cheeks and telling himself it wasn't beyond him to learn something new today, Albert tentatively began to type. Margot made humming noises while she filled out the form and with the decisive click to retract the nib of her pen, she shunted back her chair and got to her feet.

"Right, I'll just take this back and see how long they think it will take them to find the information."

Staring at the screen, his two index fingers gainfully employed to type a simple question, Albert didn't look up when he asked, "Should I come with you?"

"No, I don't suppose I will be more than a few seconds." Her prediction proved to be true, Margot returning less than a minute later with an annoyed look on her face. "What I wouldn't give to use a stun gun on that woman," she complained grumpily, dropping into the chair next to Albert.

"Valerie?"

"Yes, Valerie. I guarantee you she has that information immediately available and to hand, but she cannot possibly get it until she has processed the form. She asked that I return in half an hour just to mess me about."

Finally finished entering the prompt, 'American artist' Albert hit the button to translate it.

"The two of you do not get along?" he hazarded.

"We went to school together and she was a foul little cow even then. I gave her a speeding ticket on my first day in the job which caused a huge fight. She *was* speeding but she screamed at me in the street, accusing me of picking on her. Mercifully, I had the evidence to back up the ticket, but she hates me, so if she can find a way to get back at me, petty as it might be, Valerie Roussel is going to do it ."

Filing the information away, Albert said, "Um, what do I do with this now?"

"You need to highlight the prompt, right click on it, then copy and paste it into the village archive."

"Ah," Albert expressed joy at the simplicity of the task, yet with his fingers poised above the keyboard, he asked, "Just two small things. What does right click mean? And how do I copy and paste something?"

Amused, Margot snorted a laugh. "Perhaps I should tackle the research element by myself."

Albert pulled an apologetic face. "Yes, I think that might be best." Of course, that left Albert with nothing much to do at all, and feeling a bit like a fifth wheel, he decided to see if he couldn't charm the two ladies in the village hall into hurrying up their delivery of the information Margot requested.

Margot wished him luck, her fingers flying over the keyboard to her front as she interrogated the village archive for information about the mysterious American artist.

Chapter 37

Celeste could feel the neat whisky burning its way into her gut and regretted drinking it already. Convinced she needed something to settle her nerves, she had poured a double measure and downed it in one gulp.

Her conversation with Captain Allard did not go according to plan and her concern that events were spiralling out of control and about to get even worse were higher now than they had been before. The burden of her secret had always sat heavily, yet she had kept it for five decades out of love and wanted nothing more than to keep it from ever reaching the ears of the one person she felt an overwhelming need to protect.

If the truth came out it would change the way *everyone* looked at her, but she didn't care about them. There was only one person whose opinion mattered and desperate for some reassurance, she chose to make a phone call.

When the call ended, she felt a little better, though the neat whisky still burned in her stomach.

The Swedish archaeologists had left the village. It was a relief, but more than a little too late. Had they left two days ago, their colleague would not have been killed, and the body in the field would never have been discovered. Those who knew of his existence would have quietly and carefully filled in the excavations made by the Swedish team and perhaps nothing more would ever have been said.

Yet none of that happened, and the worst part of it, if one ignored the horror of their secret bubbling so close to the surface, was that somewhere among her group of conspirators a killer lurked. One of their number chose to kill Bjorn Ironfoundersson, taking a rock to his head when all they discussed was the option of a few veiled, anonymous threats.

But was it actually one of her group? Celeste had been questioning that very assumption since last night and the fear that she might be right was like a fiery rock in her core. It was too awful to believe, and threw into doubt everything she thought she knew.

That was why the person she called was on his way to her house.

Chapter 38

Albert offered the ladies in the village hall his most winning smile.

"Hello," he hallooed them. "Sorry, but my French isn't particularly good. My name is Albert, and this is Rex." He introduced his dog, who dutifully wagged his tail.

"*Got anything to eat?*" asked Rex. "*I could do with a snack. I'm getting a little hungry. Usually my human stops for lunch at the public house and that's almost always good for a few titbits.*"

Simone and Valerie glanced down at the dog and back up at Albert. Sensing that they were not dog people, Albert pressed on.

"I was rather hoping to find out a little more about that archaeological dig. I know Margot only just submitted the paperwork, but it is rather a pressing matter." He took out his wallet. "Is there a charity to which I can donate?" he asked, the subtext in his question about as clear as he could make it without actually saying, 'would you like a bribe?'.

Valerie started to protest but her mother cut over the top to say, "There is a one hundred Euro fee for inquiries to be expedited." Her eyes were locked on Albert's wallet.

Wondering how many other people got tapped up when they wanted information, Albert handed over five crisp twenty Euro notes. The money vanished almost instantly, Simone taking it with her as she returned to the filing cabinets behind the counter. From the third drawer down, about halfway back, she removed a cardboard drop file and from within it a thin cardboard folder.

Returning to the table where she'd been working with her daughter, Simone opened the folder and placed it facing toward Albert.

Albert needed to fish out his reading glasses to scrutinise the small text, but of course it was all in French and most of the words he could not decipher.

Looking back up at Simone, he asked, "Can I take this away with me just for a moment?"

"No, you cannot," snapped Valerie without pausing for thought.

"Yes, you can," replied Simone, contradicting her daughter. "There is, however," she added quickly just as Albert was lifting the folder from the table, "a small fee to remove documents from the village council offices."

Albert almost laughed. Having opened the door to handing over money, Simone was angling to get her hands on some more. Perhaps she was going to make sure it went to a good cause, but he rather suspected the good cause would be whatever she decided to spend it on.

Rather than get ripped off for a second time in as many minutes, Albert unclipped Rex's lead.

Rex looked up at his human expectantly.

"Fetch Margot for me would you, please, Rex?"

Pleased to have something to do, Rex bounded back across the room. The door offered him a little bit of trouble, but it was furnished with a long handle not a round knob, so demonstrating his dexterity, Rex jumped up onto his back legs to operate it.

"Ha! Take that humans and your stupid doors."

The door opened outward and he dropped to the floor to scurry through it. Finding Margot on the other side where they had left her, Rex nudged her arm with his nose.

"Can you come with me, please? You are needed in the other room."

Margot wasn't getting anywhere with her searching so far. Starting with the words 'American' and 'artist', she had hoped to get an immediate hit. However the search returned nothing so she had gone back fifty years and was making her way through all the newspaper clippings, photographs, and entries from that time.

With Rex's nose leaving damp marks on the sleeve of her coat, at which she frowned, she asked, "Where's Albert?"

"*In the other room,*" Rex explained, doing his best to keep his tone patient.

Failing to understand what he wanted, Margot scratched the fur around Rex's head and went back to reading through the archive pages.

Seeing that more direct action was required Rex took the arm of her chair between his teeth and began to drag it backwards.

Margot attempted to grip hold of the desk to remain in place, but Rex's low centre of gravity and four pawed traction won the battle easily, Dragging the wheeled chair five feet before Margot managed to get out of it.

"Would you like me to come with you by any chance?" she asked.

Rex danced about and wagged his tail. "*Finally! And they say humans can't be taught.*"

He let Margot get the door this time - they were far harder to open inward - but bounded through ahead of her to show his human what he had achieved.

"*I got her.*"

Albert showed Margot the form. Valerie was in the corner of the room by the filing cabinets where she could ignore what was going on, and Simone looked grumpy to have been denied an additional chance to rinse money from Albert.

"The ladies were kind enough to find the appropriate paperwork for me," Albert announced, generously brushing over the truth of the matter. "It's a bit tricky for me to read though." Despite his claim, Albert had been leafing through it while he waited for Rex to reappear with Margot and had discovered what he believed to be the motion opposing the dig attached to the back of the first form with a paper clip.

There was just one name on it. A name that he found both surprising and a little disturbing, yet he chose to wait until Margot had the chance to look at the paperwork herself before pointing it out.

He lapsed into silence, impatiently waiting for Margot to read through the form she now held.

Her eyes skimming over it, Margot muttered, "this was only submitted a few weeks before they arrived and started to dig." She glanced up from the form to look at Simone. "Is that normal?" she asked. "They got approval that fast? It hardly seems like there was enough time for anyone to oppose it."

Simone's cheeks coloured slightly, her eyes twitching across to look at Albert, then just as swiftly looking away when she found his knowing expression aimed her way.

"They paid a fee to have their application expedited, did they?" Albert sneered just a little. "Is that why the motion to oppose their application was denied?"

Valerie came storming back across the room, the thunderous expression on her face sufficient to assure Albert she was going to deny the accusation on her mother's behalf, but he didn't need to hear the truth to feel certain it was so.

"How dare you …" Valerie began, her full head of steam ready to rebuke Albert for his insolence until Margot shot her down.

"Be quiet!" Her raised voice silenced Valerie in an instant. Looking from daughter to mother and back again, she asked, "You're taking bribes, aren't you?"

Their mouths were clamped shut, but their expressions told the truth and Albert said, "I can testify to being a hundred Euros lighter."

Gritting her teeth, Margot growled, "Hand it back. Right now." She wanted to arrest them both, just because it would make her feel good, but slapping cuffs on them would be overkill, and she didn't have any with her anyway.

Looking down her nose, Valerie sneered, "You can't tell us what to do. You're not a police officer."

"Yes, I am," Margot snapped. "Suspended is not the same as fired and the crime remains a crime regardless."

Simone made urgent motions that her daughter should do as Margot suggested; she didn't want their little enterprise exposed.

Valerie looked fit to burst, veins standing out on her forehead as she fought to keep her mouth shut.

Narrowing her eyes, Margot said, "Be thankful I have no time to deal with this today ladies, but rest assured, there will be an investigation." She held their gaze for several seconds, daring either woman to challenge her.

When both showed the good sense to stay quiet, Margot repeated her earlier command, "Give Mr Smith back his money."

Simone silently returned to the filing cabinet and while she retrieved his cash, Albert reached across to the paperwork still held in Margot's hands, flicking the first few pages over to get to the attached form at the back.

"I think this is the motion to oppose, Margot. Do you see the name of the person who signed it?"

Margot's eyes once again flipped left and right as she moved them down the page looking for the information she required. It was indeed the motion to oppose which had been proposed and then seconded.

When she saw the names, her eyes almost popped from her head.

Chapter 39

Away from the two women in the village hall, Albert and Margot discussed what to do with their new information.

"I'm going to ask her directly," Albert remarked. He'd asked his landlady what she knew about the Swedish archaeologists and their dig, and she had lied at every opportunity. It was Celeste's name on the paperwork, her motion to oppose the dig. She concealed her involvement quite deliberately and it made Albert question what other lies she might have conjured.

"I'll come with you," Margot grabbed hold of the mouse at the computer terminal, intending to shut it down.

Albert stopped her. "There's no need. I just want to ask her a few questions and I think I can handle one little old lady in her eighties. Whoever killed Bjorn and then attacked me, it wasn't Celeste Darroze; she just doesn't have the physical strength and I don't see how she could have evaded Rex through those gardens. She's probably not going to tell me the truth anyway, so I think it might be best if you continue researching the village archives here. I'll aim to be back in half an hour or so."

Margot saw the sense in Albert's plan yet felt it was necessary to remind him that he'd been attacked less than twenty-four hours ago.

"I'll be more wary, my dear, I promise you. And I'll have Rex with me. He's dangerous enough to put most people off."

Margot still didn't like it, but she let it go, agreeing with Albert that if they were going to find answers there was a distinct possibility it would be hidden in the village archive. Before he could leave, she had one final question to ask.

"What do we do about Captain Allard? He countersigned the application to oppose the dig. Surely, that means he is even more involved than you first thought."

Albert didn't like it, but he had to agree. The local police chief had been acting strangely since he first met him, but he was too young to have had anything to do with the murder of the American artist and had a convincing alibi for the time of Albert's attack - he was busy berating Margot.

"Involved, yes," Albert agreed. "But we know he didn't kill the man fifty years ago."

Her voice quiet as if uttering something she wished she didn't have to say, Margot pointed out, "But he could have killed Bjorn Ironfoundersson."

Albert clicked his tongue at Rex to let him know that it was time to go, but paused before departing to give Margot an answer.

"If that's the case, then we're in a lot more trouble than we think."

Chapter 40

To create the diversion he believed he needed, Lars had left the dig site and the promise of what lay beneath the ground to make his way into the village. There he knocked on the door of Marion Perrault. He knew she was a police officer because Bjorn had invested an inordinate amount of time attempting to talk her knickers off the night after they arrived in the village.

She had been in the bar with some of her colleagues, a bunch of them out for a drink after work. It was because Bjorn had succeeded in his quest and Lars had needed to track him down the following morning that he knew where to find her.

His only concern when approaching her house was that she might still be at work or out somewhere else. However, the lights shining from within as the day around him darkened, suggested he was in luck.

When she opened the door, her face showed the surprise she felt to find the Swedish archaeologist on her doorstep.

Lars had prepared for the moment, fixing a haunted expression on his face in readiness to deliver the lie he'd concocted.

"I thought you had all left?" Marion expressed her confusion. Word of their departure had gone round the village mere minutes after they checked out of their lodgings that morning.

Whispering, and getting in close so that she could hear what he had to say, Lars said, "I can explain all that later. I have information about what happened to Bjorn and I need to speak to you."

Surprised by his revelation, Marion recovered quickly. Assuming her role as a police officer, she said, "let me get my coat. We should go to the station."

This was exactly what Lars hoped for, and watching her don her winter gear he fingered the knife in his pocket.

Chapter 41

The temperature outside had dropped significantly, the winter sun setting early so close to the solstice. It wasn't quite dark, but it was far from light out. Huffing and puffing as he walked briskly to get back to the guest house, Albert ran through his head all that he knew about what was going on in La Obrey.

It didn't amount to very much. However, now that he was thinking about it, while he could rule out Captain Allard playing any part in the murder of the American artist, the same could not be said about Celeste.

Her age dictated that she would have been a young woman at the time of his death. Combine with the fact that she had lied to him about her knowledge of the application to dig being opposed and she suddenly became a credible suspect. But who was the man buried in the field and why would Celeste want to kill him? Equally, Albert wanted to know how it was that anyone else in the village could be involved.

Approaching the guest house, Albert jolted when a plausible answer presented itself. If the young Celeste had indeed stabbed and killed the American, it was possible she had done so in self-defence. There was, after all, just the one wound to the victim. Perhaps he had attacked her and the knife was his. It was nothing more than a loose working theory, but it went some way to explaining how it could be that there were so many people involved in the conspiracy.

Hugo at the coffee shop had to be close to her age and there were other people he'd seen her talking to who would then glance surreptitiously in his direction. Captain Allard still didn't fit the picture, but his father might. The family had a long policing tradition; that was what he heard, and who better to call when a young woman had been attacked than the local police?

Albert paused outside the door to allow himself a moment to think things through once more. He unclipped Rex from his lead, giving himself two free hands to undo the laces on his boots.

Rex was not enjoying the cold; the frigid air bothered his nostrils and for the last several minutes of their walk he been steadfastly breathing through his mouth to avoid worsening the chill in his nose. Only now that they were on the doorstep of the guest house and sheltered from the worst of it did he think to sample the air.

His eyes dilated and his brain kicked into high gear at the exact same moment Albert leaned over him to open the door.

With a bark of, "*He's here!*" Rex barged through the door, sending it flying from Albert's grip to slam against the wall inside with a loud bang.

"Rex!" Albert shouted after his dog, but the oversized German shepherd was already vanishing around the first corner. Hurriedly kicking off his boots and cursing at the amount of snow he brought in with him, Albert gave chase.

He'd seen Rex turn left to go through the dining room, and followed him that way. Running past the table he spotted a familiar looking coat draped over one of the chairs. His brain insisted he recognised it and somehow knew the owner, but too focused on catching his errant dog, he didn't give it a second look.

The echo of Rex barking ferociously boomed through the house. It was a type of bark that Albert could recognise as one that indicated violence might shortly ensue. With no idea what might have gotten into him, Albert ran, his socked feet slipping on the floorboards.

Rex was searching the house as fast as he could. He didn't know whether it was the fourth or fifth time now that he had pursued the same scent, but the strength of it told him the man he sought was in the house right now. All he had to do was find him. Do that and he could put a stop to any thoughts he might have about hurting his human.

He could hear Albert shouting his name and was glad of it. He sounded annoyed and that meant he hadn't come to any harm yet.

With the exception of the kitchen, the doors in the downstairs of the house were not locked. This gave Rex the opportunity to run wherever he wished, his nose down and his hackles up as he tracked a man he believed to be a killer.

Reaching the bottom of the stairs, he found the scent to be equally powerful in both directions. Cursing under his breath he took a fifty, fifty gamble and went up.

Meanwhile downstairs, Albert was having a spot of bother. Racing through the house in pursuit of his dog, he'd slipped on a hardwood floor as he came into a drawing room. Arms flailing, his right hand came to rest on a sideboard. He expected the heavy piece of furniture to stay put, yet it shifted an inch and that was sufficient to spill the ornaments decorating its top surface.

Panicking, for there were a dozen small porcelain dog figurines all threatening to topple and fall, Albert scrambled to stop them. This only made things worse, several expletives bursting from his lips when his desperate fingers mis-timed his grab for a wobbling springer spaniel and sent it flying. Before his eyes it careened into two other figurines and like a cue ball it sent them flying too.

Spreading his arms like a barrier, he was able to stop all but one from leaping to its death, but as that sailed over the edge and plunged to the floor, he stuck out a foot to give it something soft to hit.

It cracked against his big toe painfully, bounced off, and rolled beneath the sideboard. From the sound of it, Albert believed it was still in one piece. Rex had stopped barking, so praying that he had a few seconds to spare, Albert made sure the remaining figurines on top of the sideboard were going to remain where they were and got down on his knees to collect the one he dropped.

Ironically, the figurine in question was that of a German shepherd. With one side of his face pressed against the floor, Albert reached under the sideboard to pick it up. Once he had it clasped in his hand and could find no sign that it had chipped or broken, he started to get up and it was then that he spotted something else.

He stared, questioning his eyeballs. Were they really seeing what he thought they were? The figurine forgotten, Albert clambered back to his feet, gripped the edges of the sideboard, and putting his back into it, levered one end away from the wall.

The figurines on top, the few that had remained standing, toppled and spilled, three of them crashing to the floor where they broke. Not that Albert noticed.

He was staring at the floor behind the sideboard. What he had believed was a carpet was in fact a large rug that covered almost the entire surface area of the room. Almost but not quite. Where it failed to quite touch the wall behind the sideboard, half an inch of the surface beneath was still visible.

Not surprised that Celeste would want to hide the old linoleum, it was such a garish kaleidoscopic array of colours, it was undeniably the same as the piece he found embedded in the American artist's shoe.

There could be no question that he was looking at the same piece of floor and he suspected that were he to lift the rug, which was trapped beneath several pieces of furniture, he would find a piece missing from where a body was dragged backwards across it.

As another piece of the mystery slotted into place, Albert backtracked through the house, playing through his mind the other clues he'd seen today. The blood-soaked handkerchief bearing Celeste's initials and the piece of green thread were two that jumped out.

In the dining room, he stopped where the coat was draped over the back of the chair. It was the dull metallic red coat worn by the man he ran into the previous morning. They met by the trees, not far from where Bjorn's body had been discovered and right after the man in the green coat ran away.

The man in the green coat had seemed to vanish and now he knew how. Albert took the coat off the chair and opened it out. The inside lining was a dark green, and when he pulled out the right sleeve he found the round silver badge he recalled seeing just below the shoulder seam. Yet more damning, just below it was a repair made with the same dark green thread he took from Celeste's elbow a few hours ago.

Whoever owned the coat had been watching where Bjorn's body was found and later tried to kill Albert.

"Figured it all out, have you?" asked Celeste, stepping through the doorway and into the room.

Chapter 42

Working the dispatch desk when a garbled, panicked call came in, Gerard Mansart tried to get the name of the person claiming to have seen a police officer being attacked. They had a distinctive accent, though their French was close to flawless, but the caller hung up before any personal information could be obtained.

Regardless that the call was anonymous, it could not be ignored. One of their own was in grave peril and the caller even gave a name: Marion Perrault. The caller claimed to have seen her fighting with an old man. He had a bald head and large German Shepherd dog. He thought he might have spoken with an English accent.

Lars enjoyed the chance to frame the meddlesome Englishman. It probably wouldn't stick – he would likely have an alibi to vouch for his whereabouts, but that didn't matter. The point was to send the police to find their fallen colleague and to rush around the village looking for Albert Smith. If they were doing that they wouldn't notice what he was doing and he watched with triumph when the kid they'd left guarding the dig site was called away.

The cops would rush around, dealing with the murdered police officer and all the drama that went with such a terrible event, leaving Lars free to dig a big hole. And that is precisely what he did, his pickaxe striking the earth almost before the police officer in his squad car was out of sight.

The partially frozen ground proved easier to excavate than he'd expected, large clumps of dirt coming out with each shovel stroke. Less than five minutes after breaking ground, the tip of his tool struck something solid. Something solid that sounded hollow and his work rate increased from desperate to feverish.

He wanted nothing more than to get what he came for and leave. For him La Obrey would forever hold terrible memories.

Lars had to stop to remove his coat. Despite the cold he was sweating and getting hotter by the minute. Stripping it off, he threw it to one side, and went straight back to work clearing as much dirt from the surface of the metal crate as he could.

When he found an edge, he cleared around it. He didn't need to get the crate out of the ground and knew he wouldn't be able to lift it anyway. All he needed to do was get it open. There was a wheelbarrow in the back of his van and space inside for him to load everything he hoped to find.

When finally, after a further ten minutes of sweating, grunting, and striving, he finally managed to lever the lid up, the meagre moonlight shining down through the denuded tree branches reflected a soft orange glow back up onto his face. There, a grin that would startle the Cheshire Cat was now fixed in place.

Chapter 43

Margot's eyes were beginning to hurt. One of the drivers for her wanting a job that had her out and about and not in an office in front of a screen was that she loathed computer work. She accepted that some degree of it was inevitable even as a police officer but the hours she spent chained to a terminal were measured in single figures a week where most of her friends could boast as many hours each day.

She had yet to be scrutinising the village archive for so much as thirty minutes, but the small text size forced her to squint repeatedly. Trawling through page after page of banal reports that were probably only interesting to those who appeared in the accompanying pictures was mind numbing. Regardless, telling herself that Albert would shortly return, and hoping that when he did she would either have something to show him, or at the very least the confidence to say there was nothing to find, she forced herself to continue.

Scrolling to the next page - she had now reached the June of the year after she started her search - she found a picture of a wedding. A petite bride stood next to a tall man, both showing broad smiles. It was more of the same nonsense she'd been looking at for the past half an hour.

She scrolled the wheel on the mouse again, moving on to the next page which was when her brain caught up with her and she hastily scrolled back.

She hadn't bothered to read any of the words beneath the picture in the article that accompanied the photograph of the new husband and wife. The bride looked vaguely familiar, yet it was the man's face at which she was now gaping.

She had never seen it before, but she had seen its likeness at the coroner's office when Daniel showed her the 3D approximation of the victim's face. Daniel remarked at the time how the technology had grown quite accurate over the years, but the resemblance was uncanny.

Certain she had now found their mysterious American artist she skimmed her eyes over the words beneath the photograph and her jaw dropped open.

The husband and wife were named as Steve and Celeste Cattrell and now Margot knew why the bride looked familiar. The graininess of the black and white photograph made it harder to discern, but the bride was Celeste Darroze, a woman everyone knew as a childless spinster.

Just behind her to the right, a man she recognised as Captain Allard's father, the former chief of police before his son took over, was holding a little boy in his arms – Maxwell Allard as he was then. She guessed his age to be maybe two. She also recognised Celeste's sister, Marguerite, who stood next to a man who had his arm around her and two children.

Margot could not recall the name of Marguerite's husband and believed he had died many years ago when she was very little. Marguerite was gone too, lost to cancer more than ten years ago, but staring at the two children huddled against her legs, a question formed inside Margot's head, and it demanded an answer.

She knew the children. They were grown now and in their fifties. Anton and Lucille were brother and sister, but there was something undeniably off about that. They were not twins – Margot didn't know how she knew that, but she did – but they were too close in age to be brother and sister.

Leaving the photograph and article on the computer, she jumped across to the second terminal where she started a new search. She wanted to look at births recorded in the village gazette four to five years before the wedding.

With a jolt, she saw the need to tell Albert. He was on his way to speak with Celeste, heck he had to be there by now unless he'd been delayed somehow, and this was information he needed to know.

Chapter 44

"I didn't mean to kill him," Celeste made her way to the nearest chair and sat in it, her head and eyes down to look at the surface of the dining table. Anything was better than meeting Albert's eyes.

Albert's phone started to ring. His coat was in the entrance lobby along with his boots, discarded when he came in from the cold to the toasty warm house. He wanted to get it, but Celeste had just confessed to murder and his need to hear her story won out.

Above his head, the sound of Rex's paws running down a corridor echoed through the ceiling.

With a slow breath Albert took a moment to steady himself and slipped into his old detective mode. He chose to remain standing, taking up a position opposite Celeste at the other end of the table.

His voice gentle, he said, "Tell me what happened."

Celeste appeared to have shrunk to half her former size. Wretched and afraid, her arms were clamped in her lap, her shoulders hunched and slumped, and she would not look up. Albert thought he would have to push her to reveal the full story, but he was wrong.

"He was never violent before we were married. It started on our wedding night."

Albert's phone rang off and started to ring again almost immediately.

Agitated, he felt sure the call would be important and that it was almost certainly from Margot. Had she found in the village archive the information he was now learning? Celeste was not a spinster, she had been married. Married to an evil man who she killed one night. Unwilling to move lest he break the spell and the landlady stop talking, he stayed where he was, listening impassively.

"I begged him to stop, but he said I needed to learn my place, to understand the consequences of disappointing him."

"He hit you?" Albert wanted to confirm.

Celeste didn't reply straight away, but after a couple of seconds she nodded, and her response crept out as a painful whisper. "He did. Not all the time and he was always apologetic afterwards if he could see I was truly hurt."

"How long did that continue?" Albert asked, the question a subtle variation on the question he was really asking, 'What happened to make you kill him?'

"Less than two weeks. That's how long we were married." She shuddered and seemed to shrink a little further. "I never meant to kill him, but …" She lapsed into silence, unable to complete the sentence.

"Yes?" Albert prompted and she finally looked up to meet his eyes.

Her face grim, there was no regret or remorse when she said, "But I'm glad he's dead."

Chapter 45

Rex's nose was never wrong, but sometimes it could become confused. The scent of the man he wanted to chase was all over the house. It was strong and fresh to make it clear he was either here right now or had only just left.

Rex believed the former. He'd found the man's coat and knew humans, delicate creatures that they are, are wont to wear as many extra layers as possible when it is cold.

At the foot of the stairs and faced with a choice, he'd gone up, following the man's smell, but it led him to the door of the room in which he and his human were staying. That confused him even more.

The man was in his room?

Rex got down on his belly to snuffle under the gap at the bottom of the door. Sucking in a fat noseful of air, he sampled and sorted it before deciding that the man had been inside but was no longer there.

Back on his paws, Rex scouted around, quickly confirming to himself that the man was not upstairs. With that in mind, he ran back the way he had come. His human was downstairs somewhere, though Rex could no longer hear him shouting his name, but if the killer was still in the guesthouse and wasn't on the upper floor ...

With singular purpose, he returned to the ground floor and reaching it he saw his quarry. The man he'd chased the previous night was right in front of him, framed in the light coming through the front door at the far end of the hallway running through the guesthouse.

With a bark of determination, Rex launched into a sprint.

Chapter 46

"Captain Allard," he snapped the reply into his phone. Why were they bothering him now? He was off duty and had expressly instructed that he only be contacted in the event of a dire emergency.

"Sir," the voice of Alain Sauvage, one of the only senior officers to whom he was not related, came filled with apology and adrenalin, plus something else Captain Allard couldn't yet identify. "It's Marion Perrault, Sir."

"What about her?" he growled impatiently, seconds away from chewing the man out for bothering him with whatever petty nonsense this would prove to be.

"She's been murdered, Sir."

Captain Allard blinked, his mouth unable to form a response. At least he could now identify the underlying tone in his subordinate's voice, it was horror.

"Sir?" Sauvage checked his boss was still there. "Did you hear me, Sir? Marion Perrault's body is lying by the side of the river at the park. She's been stabbed, Sir."

What was happening? How could one of his officers be dead? They didn't get crime in La Obrey and what little did occur could all be classed as misdemeanours.

Forcing his tongue to operate, he managed to stammer, "Who found her?"

"Vincent Bruni, Sir. He heard the call come in and went straight there. Everyone is there now, Sir. Do we seal off the village?"

"Hmmm? What was that?" Captain Allard was only half listening. His mind swirled with the news, but his thoughts were not about who might have perpetrated the crime and how to catch them, but whether he still had time to do what needed to be done tonight. He had to go to the scene. How could he not? But dealing with Margot and the troublesome old Englishman had to take priority. They were so close to the truth that if he didn't remove them now they would expose it all.

"The roads into and out of town, Sir. We need to seal them off to stop her killer from escaping and only you have the authority to give that order."

"Yes, of course ... Wait! No, not yet," If he closed the roads now what would he do with Margot's body? The old man would fall down some stairs; that was easy enough and if he could convince everyone that Bjorn Ironfoundersson's death was an accident, Albert Smith's would be a cinch. But Margot's body had to go somewhere and he wasn't about to bury it in Drucker's Field, that was for certain. "Not yet," he repeated, his brain working at high speed to factor in all the elements he needed to consider.

"But what if he gets away, Sir?" Sauvage wasn't used to challenging his boss. Actually, he didn't think he had ever questioned his orders before, but Captain Allard's command made no sense.

Picking up on the way Sauvage phrased the question, Captain Allard said, "Wait. Do we know who the killer is?"

"Yes, Sir. At least, we have a prime suspect. We received an anonymous call in which we discovered the attack on Marian Perrault. The same caller described Albert Smith as her attacker. He even said the dog was with him."

Growling out his response, Captain Allard commanded, "Then find him and arrest him, man."

Sauvage snapped out a quick, "Yes Sir," but Captain Allard had already hung up.

He was in front of the library building sitting in his car. Tracking her down proved simple enough; Celeste overheard her discussing their next destination with Albert Smith. His leg twitched with impatience – he wanted to get on with the grisly task, but he couldn't go in to get Margot without someone seeing him with her, so he was waiting for her to come out.

Chapter 47

"Where are you, Albert?" Margot gripped her phone and begged the person at the other end to pick up. She had called his number four times now and sent him three text messages. He wasn't answering and she was beginning to fear the worst.

Redialling, she called the station and to her horror found it was answered by Curtis Allard.

Grimacing, she pushed on. "Curtis, I need you to listen."

"And why would I do that?" he sneered.

"Because I think Celeste Darroze killed the man they found in the shallow grave in Drucker's Field."

The laugh from Curtis sounded genuine. "Don't be so stupid. That old lady never hurt a fly. What are you doing investigating it anyway? You're suspended, remember? In fact, I think you are probably fired, Margot. At least, you will be when I tell my father you are still disobeying his orders."

"She's his wife" Margot blurted.

She got a moment of hung nothingness before Curtis asked, "Who is whose wife?"

"Celeste!" Margot yelled into the phone. "Celeste was married to a man called Steve Cattrell. That's who was found in the shallow grave and given that everyone in La Obrey believes she is a spinster, I think it likely that she killed him."

"What are you talking about, you daft cow? How about this? No one cares about the body you found this morning because Marion Perrault was murdered this afternoon and your new friend Albert Smith did it."

Stunned, Margot could only say, "What?"

Curtis sounded triumphant when he next spoke, as though he was pleased to have such awful news to share.

"Yes, he was seen stabbing her in the park. Is he with you now?"

"No," Margot murmured, now questioning if she couldn't raise Albert because he had just killed one of her best friends. It couldn't be true though. Why would Albert kill Marion? He didn't even know her.

"Are you sure? Where are you?" Curtis pushed for answers.

Confused by the diabolical turn of events, horrified that the news of Marion's death might be true, yet convinced the report of Albert's involvement would be wholly inaccurate, she thumbed the red button to end her call, cutting Curtis off before he could say another word.

Bewildered, she looked at the computer screen again.

Anton and Lucille were known as siblings, but they were not born of the same parents. Anton was Celeste's, but he was raised by her sister and brother-in-law and to Margot's knowledge had nothing to do with his birth mother.

Clearly that had something to do with her husband and his murder. Steve Cattrell was not Anton's father; the box on the birth certificate was listed as 'unknown' yet Anton's age dictated that she was a woman when she gave birth, not a girl who might, at that time, have been expected to hide the pregnancy and give up the child.

Regardless of the fine details and what bearing they might have on Steve Cattrell's death, she needed to warn Albert. Not just about Celeste, but that the police would be looking for him. How long could it be until they came knocking on the guesthouse door?

Stuffing her phone back into her coat pocket, Margot didn't even pause to power down the computers, something a sign above each monitor requested each user do before leaving.

She was in too much of a hurry.

Racing from the library and into the frozen landscape outside, she slipped on the icy surface, her feet skating for a second before she found purchase. The urgency of her quest demanded speed, but her car was on her drive and going on foot there was no safe way to run.

It wasn't far though; she could get to the guesthouse in just a few minutes.

Setting off, she sensed rather than heard or saw the person behind her, but in trying to turn her body to see who it was, she caught a glimpse of something coming at her neck and the world went blank.

Captain Allard looked around to be certain no one had seen and slipped the stun gun away. Killing Margot brought him no joy; he wished there was any other solution, but she refused to heed his instructions and had brought about her own demise. It had to be this way.

The family shame would stop with him.

Chapter 48

Rex charged, head up, teeth bared, and violence on his mind. His favourite part of police training had always been the game of chase and bite. The humans would cheat by donning padded suits, which forced Rex to get inventive. They would offer an arm that he could bite with all his might without achieving any harm to the person inside.

What good was that?

Rex learned their tricks on his first day and thereafter found something to bite that was not protected. His handlers disapproved. Quite vehemently, Rex discovered, but he played the game the way he believed it was supposed to be played and made no apology afterward.

Just as he suspected, when training finished, the people he was sent to chase wore no protective suits and he was the only one of his class prepared for the squealing and bleeding their targets chose to emit.

Chase and bite had almost always been a game for Rex. A fun game at that, but right now things were different. The target to his front had tried to kill his human, an old man he really liked, and it was payback time.

Hitting full speed, he timed his leap. The man had hardly moved an inch. Backed against the front door, he appeared to be petrified by fear.

Rex launched himself but as his front paws left the floor he realised his error.

The man wasn't frozen in place, he'd been biding his time.

Moving fast, the man yanked the guesthouse front door open. Using it as a shield to hide behind, he flattened himself to the wall and pulled the solid piece of wood in tight to his body.

Unable to stop, Rex flew straight past him out of the open door and into the snow outside which was just beginning to fall again.

The sound of the door slamming shut reached his ears before his paws hit the ground and skidding to a stop he turned to find his re-entry barred.

He barked, angry to be beaten so easily, but stopped a few seconds later. The man wasn't about to let him back in, and assuming he still had ill intent in mind meant Rex's human was in danger.

He needed to find another way and he had to be quick about it.

Chapter 49

Albert heard Rex bark, the loud noise muffled by the closed dining room door, but it gave him reassurance that his dog was still in the house. He also noted that his phone had not rung for more than a minute, the incessant caller either giving up or finding a solution of their own. He still wanted to check it, but there was no way to do that right now.

Celeste was laying it all out, telling him what happened and why. The night she stabbed her husband he had come home drunk. He was becoming thoroughly unpopular in La Obrey and had started fights in several bars in the short time they were together.

That night was no exception, and having found himself facing off against three men when his need to voice opinion on any subject he chose riled the bar clientele to breaking point, he came home bruised and angry. So angry that when he knocked her down for the umpteenth time and she refused to apologise for existing, he decided to show her a real lesson – he would take it out on her son.

It wasn't his son after all.

Celeste said she couldn't remember picking up the knife, but she chased him through the house, intercepting her husband at Anton's bedroom.

Albert tried to keep his lips shut when the revelation of her child occurred. Not only was she married, but she had a son. Who better to carry out the recent crimes on behalf of the elderly woman?

"Where is he now, Celeste?"

The door opened behind Albert, and he spun around to find the man in the metallic red coat entering the room. He limped heavily. Another cog slotted into place, and Albert could see it all. With a nod, Albert laughed at himself. The killer really had returned to the scene of the crime. Albert caught him watching what the police were doing. So much for clichés. He'd run away, reversed his coat, and doubled back to bluff that he was out getting exercise on doctor's orders.

Eying him warily, Albert asked, "Did you intend to kill me last night?"

From behind his back, Anton produced a knife.

Celeste cried out, "No! No, Anton!"

Anton's eyes never left Albert's, but they tightened slightly upon hearing his mother's anguished cries.

"It has to be this way, mother. You protected me when I was defenceless and now it is my turn."

Her face froze for a heartbeat, the truth of things seizing her heart like a vice.

"It was you!" she gasped. "You killed the Swedish man."

"I didn't mean to. I just wanted them to leave. I swear I didn't even hit him that hard."

"You hit him with a rock," Albert pointed out. "Then you tried to kill me."

"To keep a secret!" Anton yelled. "My mother's secret. A secret her friends kept all these years. Don't they deserve to go to their graves with their secret intact?"

"Perhaps," Albert conceded, "but not at the cost of other people's lives. Do you think they thank you for what you have done?"

Anton was shouting again in an instant. "It wasn't my fault! The archaeologist was never supposed to die. They should have packed their things and left. The secret could have stayed where it was: buried forever."

Her voice barely more than a croak, Celeste asked, "How do you even know? You were too young to remember what happened."

Anton looked at his mother with shame filled eyes. "Your sister told me. The woman I always called 'mother' revealed the truth on her deathbed. She wanted me to know what you did for me and that you had spent your life alone, playing the role of my aunt, so that no one would ever know. She said you were in a coma, and that my father's body was hidden by your friends, the shallow grave organised by Charles Allard who went on to be the chief of police. I was taken to live with my real aunt and by the time you got out of hospital I had been living with her for so long I couldn't remember you."

Celeste's eyes were filled with tears that refused to fall.

"Why did you never say anything? My sister died ten years ago, why did you never tell me what you knew."

Anton shrugged. "I tried. I wanted to. I just could never find the right time or the right words. You have been my aunt my whole life. In the end I decided to just let things be."

Celeste rose to her feet, the shame of a life of lies that hung so heavily on her soul, losing out over her need to hug her child.

Albert could see Anton wanted to go to her. He was a killer, but so was his mother. Not in the same way, but the ruination of both their lives could be traced back to the man she married. Anton would have to go to jail; there was no getting around that, but what might happen to Celeste when the truth became public knowledge he could not guess.

Anton wanted to go to his mother, but he could see the future that lay before him and had already chosen what path he must take. The secret could be protected, so far only the old man had figured it out and none of those who knew the truth – the original conspirators – would blame him for what he was about to do.

He raised the knife, advancing on Albert.

Celeste screamed, "No!" but her son wasn't listening.

Albert doubted he could outrun the younger man, even with the injury to his derriere, but he chose to give it a jolly good go.

Chapter 50

Rex was getting cold and increasingly frustrated. There were doors to get back inside the house, but none that his paws could operate. His only other choice, so far as he could see, was to go through one of the windows. He'd smashed through a couple of windows in his life, but those ones had been easier to get to.

The ground floor windows of the guesthouse were all well above his head and even with a run up, though he knew he could hit them, Rex wasn't all that confident he could do so with enough velocity to break through.

It was a good thing he didn't try it because the panes were triple glazed to keep out the winter cold and any attempt to hit them at speed would have resulted in injury or worse.

Starting to wish he had covering for his paws, Rex was about to set off on another circuit of the house when he heard the front door open. It slammed back against the wall with a loud bang, light spilling out to illuminate the snow.

Rex started forward hoping this was his chance to get back inside, but a shout from his human added urgency to his pace and his loping run became a full sprint.

In front of the guesthouse, the old man was struggling with the killer. Rex had labelled him as such from the probability that he was behind the first victim's death, but there could be no doubt now. He had a knife and was trying to stab his human with it.

Albert parried the blade away again. Racing through the house to get away from Anton, it was only his quick thinking that had kept him alive this long. Knowing he would be right on his heels, Albert swept the contents of the dining table into his path, then yanked over a bookcase as he passed it. Right by the door he'd managed to snag an umbrella and was now wielding it like a sword to keep the murderous, stab-happy Anton at bay.

It wasn't a tactic that would keep him alive for long and in the same moment that he acknowledged that probability, Anton stopped trying to stick Albert with the knife and grabbed the umbrella. He ripped it from his grip, almost pulling the old man off balance when he tried in vain to keep hold.

Discarding it with a triumphant sneer, Anton raised the knife again.

"Stop it!" Celeste screamed. She was at the front door, pale, shrivelled, tiny, and totally ignored. "This has to end, Anton!"

Anton's eyes bored into Albert's. "Oh, I'm about to end it all right."

He extended his right arm, advancing on Albert who had nowhere to go.

Had there been anyone within earshot who could translate his bark, they would have heard Rex shout, "*Round three, bitch!*" when he leapt into the air.

Rex's teeth bit down into the soft flesh of Anton's right forearm, his weight and momentum carrying the limb across and down to yank the man off his feet.

Anton dropped the knife even before his face hit the snow, his barely human squeal filling the frigid night air.

Rex dug into the frozen ground with his claws, finding his grip to then wrench his head to one side and then the other. He did it again and again, making sure the man stayed down this time. Only when he felt his human's hand on his shoulder did Rex pause to listen for a command.

Albert collected the knife, moving it well out of Anton's range when he said, "That's enough now, Rex."

Rex sat back onto his haunches obediently, panting despite the cold. He didn't move away though and he refused to take his eyes off the target.

Anton was making pain-filled groaning sounds, but when his first attempt to get up was met with a deep warning growl, he slumped back to the ground and stayed there.

Celeste left the guesthouse, descending the steps carefully to get to her son.

"Oh, Anton. Oh, what have you done," she wept, falling to her knees in the snow by his side.

Still breathing heavily, Albert retrieved his phone and coat, slipping the latter over his shoulders even as he squinted to see the missed calls and messages displayed.

They were all from Margot, but the last call was more than five minutes ago. He tapped the message icon, scanning the words to confirm why she had been calling and calling. She found out the truth about Celeste, some of which was still confusing. She'd been in a coma? She managed to convince the village she had neither a son nor a husband and it stayed a secret? These things required some explanation, but first he had to let Margot know he was okay.

He thumbed the button to ring her back, but as the phone rang a frown creased his brow. Slipping his feet into his boots, not that he could do them one handed, he went back outside where Rex still watched over Anton and Celeste cried softly into the snow.

If Margot had been trying to raise him with such urgency, why hadn't she come to the guesthouse? It wasn't that far to walk. In the minutes since her last phone call there had been more than enough time to walk from the library.

Her phone switched to voicemail and Albert stopped the call, quickly thumbing the button to redial it. When it continued to ring again, he thought it would go to voicemail and felt a wave of relief when it was answered.

"Hello?" said a voice that was very much not Margot's.

Fighting his rising sense of dread, Albert replied, "Who is this, please?"

"Pierre Perret. Whose phone is this? I just found it in the bin outside the library."

Albert's breath caught in his throat. There were flashing lights coming toward the guesthouse, multiple police cars heading his way. It was an impressive response time. Especially considering he was yet to call them.

"The phone belongs to Margot Dubois. Can you see her anywhere?"

"No, sorry, there is no one here."

The police cars pulled to stop, their wheels skidding over the snow such was the speed employed to catch their colleague's killer.

Thinking perhaps a neighbour heard the commotion and called in the disturbance at the guesthouse, Albert knew that was a wrong assumption. If that were the case they would have sent one car, not the three now spilling officers into the street.

"Who am I speaking to, please?" Pierre asked. "Perhaps I can give the phone to you to give to Margot?"

"Albert. Albert Smith," Albert replied, his mind not on the conversation, but on the police coming his way. Something was amiss and he didn't like the way things were shaping up.

"Albert Smith?" Pierre repeated the name. "Oh, my God! You're the maniac who stabbed the police officer this evening!"

In a heartbeat, Albert's world closed in around him, his brain shutting out everything else as he tried to assess the sudden influx of new information. Margot was missing, her phone discarded in the trash outside the library. The police were coming for him, and since he could be one hundred percent sure Anton had nothing to do with whatever had happened to Margot, there had to be another player in the field.

And he knew just who it had to be.

Chapter 51

"Rex!" Albert bellowed, his feet moving fast as he ran out of the guesthouse. "With me!"

The suddenness and urgency in his human's voice got him moving and he was glad to no longer watch the man lying on the snow. Now that he had given up trying to fight or run away he was quite boring.

"*Where are we going?*" Rex asked, his paws twitching with excitement. The old man didn't often move as fast as he was and Rex hoped they were going to need to run somewhere just so he could warm up.

Albert couldn't believe he was about to do it, but with the police less than twenty yards away and looking very much like they had come to take him into custody, he wasn't going to risk the chance that he might be wrong. Quite how he came to be framed for the murder of a French police officer he could easily guess: Captain Allard was behind it.

The local police chief's mysterious behaviour was no longer confusing and Albert now understood his involvement with the body buried when he was just a few years old. It was his father's secret, one he must have shared at some point when he felt his son was old enough to understand. Perhaps he waited until his son took over as the police captain, but whenever it happened, Captain Allard's father used his knowledge to help cover up the murder of Celeste's husband and hide the body.

Now the current chief of police was fighting to keep the truth under wraps to prevent the shame it would bring to his family. The investigation would be huge, the press coverage massive, and Albert had come far too close to figuring it all out.

That was why Allard's officers were coming to arrest him and almost certainly why Margot's phone was in the trash. Had he done something to her already?

She had been calling Albert less than ten minutes ago, so whatever fate befell her, unless she was already dead, there was still a chance to save her.

With that thought plastered across his brain, Albert yanked a toboggan from the side of the house and ran. Shouts followed him, but he was confident they would not open fire. He wasn't visibly carrying a firearm and in a populated area any shots that missed would land somewhere. The risk was too great.

Silently praying he wasn't about to do Captain Allard's work for him and kill himself when he crashed the toboggan, Albert dropped it to the ground and leapt on board. His body protested, but the skids were pointing downhill so in theory all he had to do was hold on and he would arrive at the library.

Chapter 52

Lars was exhausted and his shoulders, back, and hips ached. His hands were blistered and he had a huge lump on his left shin where he swung the pickaxe, missed the ground, and hit his leg. None of that mattered though, it didn't even register in his consciousness.

He was leaving La Obrey in a van loaded with gold bars, silver bars, gemstones, and jewellery. It was a haul. It was a fortune. And ten percent of it was his.

His initial plan had been to take out some of the gold, just one or two bars, to keep for himself. Walter Karlsson provided an inventory of each cache he buried along with the map to find them which meant Lars' employer knew what he was supposed to return with.

In a change of heart, Lars decided it would be better to take it all back and show that not only was he a person who could overcome adversity – getting the job done even after his team abandoned the task – he was someone who could be trusted.

He would be awarded another job at a different site and maybe another one after that. He didn't know how many there were or how many teams his employer had, but the rumour was that Walter left behind more than a hundred hidden caches.

Having gained his employer's trust, Lars would find a cache that had been raided. At least, that was the report he would give; that he found the crate and it was empty.

Wending his way down the mountain path from Drucker's field, his van wallowed and felt heavy, the suspension tested by the additional weight. It pleased him.

Leaving the treacherous road leading down from the field, he flicked on his indicator and turned left on the main road. In just a few minutes the village of La

Obrey would be in his rear-view mirror, and he would never have to see the place again.

Chapter 53

Albert knew he was going to die. The toboggan, a fancy thing made from bright red plastic, ran on steel runners that could be steered from the front by a small yoke that sat between his knees. It even had a brake ... which snapped off the first time he attempted to slow his speed.

The police officers outside Celeste's guesthouse gave chase when he set off on his suicidal run to save Margot, but he left them behind no sooner than he got on board the toboggan.

It was a downhill shot almost the whole way with a flat area for the final couple of hundred yards before he would reach the library, but to get there he had to cross the main road that bisected La Obrey and there was traffic on it.

Not exactly a lot; he could only see two sets of headlights, but they were coming from opposite directions and he could calculate their rough speed to feel certain they were going to pass each other just at the point when his out-of-control toboggan flew across the road.

One or both was going to hit him and there was nothing he could do about it.

Rex had tried to keep up but even his bounding legs couldn't match the speed the toboggan was able to achieve.

Just how fast was he going? Thirty? Could a dog like Rex run at thirty miles an hour for a short burst? Albert felt certain they could so was he doing forty? More?

The cold air tore at his coat which he'd never found time to put on properly. He wanted to zip it closed, but at this point it wasn't so much to keep out the cold but so they would be able to find all his body parts after he crashed.

Chapter 54

Captain Allard had taken the backroads to get away from the library. The more obvious and direct route went past the park and the mass of officers there dealing with Marion Perrault's body. He felt awful that he wasn't with them, but also grimly aware that he now had a perfect excuse to 'accidentally' kill Albert Smith.

He wanted to know why the old man chose to kill one of his officers, but imagined he would never know the truth. If he got the chance he would shoot the old man and that would be that.

When he reached the main road, he turned right. He knew just where he was going to go and what he needed to do to get rid of Margot Dubois. The car was one that had been sitting in the police lock up park behind the station for nine months. Left behind by the owner at the end of the previous ski season, they were never coming back for the clunky, battered piece of scrap.

Margot was going to drive it over a cliff.

Across the backseat, Maxwell Allard's cross country ski gear was ready for his return journey and the gently falling snow would cover his tracks to make it seem as though he was never there.

There might be a few questions about why he was so late joining the rest of his officers in dealing with Marion's murder, but he was the captain after all. He would reveal that he was giving them a chance to operate without his leadership and lie that he'd been watching to see how they got along and who showed true leadership potential.

Yes, it was all going to work out just fine.

The main road through La Obrey had been cleared and gritted during the day but with the snow falling again he kept his speed below fifty.

Thinking contented thoughts – he wasn't a lawbreaker, but forced to do so he could feel satisfaction in the knowledge that he was good at it – he was about to start whistling a tune to himself when he caught sight of something out of the corner of his eye.

Racing down the hill was a large German Shepherd dog. There were lots of dogs in La Obrey, but oddly only one German Shepherd that he knew of. It belonged to Claude Labrouste and was a geriatric old thing, not the fine, athletic specimen he currently watched racing across the snow.

It was Albert Smith's dog, but then where was Albert Smith? He looked behind the dog, up the hill, thinking the old Englishman must be following, but finding no one there he tracked his eyes in the other direction and almost choked.

The crazy old man was belting down the hill on a sledge and going fast enough that he would die if he hit anything harder than a pillow.

What's more, Captain Allard realised with a surge of adrenalin, he was going to cross the road right in front of his car. If he just increased his speed a little he would hit him. It was beyond perfect. He guessed correctly that the police had come for him and what he was now witness to was a suspect in full flight, but whatever the case, he could mangle the old man with the car, keep on going and get rid of both Margot Dubois and the interfering old man in one fell swoop.

"My goodness I am good at this," Captain Allard chuckled to himself.

Adding pressure to the accelerator pedal, his speed crept from a safe forty-five to a risky sixty, but he wasn't looking at the speedometer needle, his eyes were glued to the old man on the red toboggan haring down the hill toward his death.

Chapter 55

Albert's face was frozen and though he was able to hold the toboggan's steering yoke, he had lost the ability to feel anything below his wrists. Idly he questioned if that would create a numbing effect so he wouldn't feel the impact.

The car was coming from his left, what looked like a van was trundling along the road from his right and he was going to go right between them to find himself squished all over the road.

It was quite the way to go, not that Albert was thinking about himself all that much. His thoughts were centred on Rex and what might become of him.

The road was right ahead of him, the vehicles closing fast.

This was it. He had three seconds to live.

Jumping aboard the toboggan, Albert expected to be able to steer and control the device. He wanted to evade the cops at the guesthouse and find Margot. He knew the police would catch him soon enough, but if Margot was in mortal danger and he could save her ... the rest of it could be worked out after they arrested him. He hadn't hurt anyone and believed he would be able to furnish alibis to account for whatever time the murdered police officer met their end.

However, while the toboggan could be sort of steered a little, it refused to slow down, so when the brake snapped off the first time he tried to use it, he was already going too fast to consider a controlled crash.

Wondering if it might be nicer to just close his eyes, they widened instead. There was a bank of snow a yard to his right. It wasn't much but it might give him a chance. Twisting the yoke, the toboggan almost flipped when it altered course at a speed the designers never expected it to achieve.

The nose hit the bank, angling up before sailing out into open air, Albert sitting on board it, his mouth open and his coat flapping like a superhero's cloak.

Acting like a take off ramp, the bank of snow kicked him up into the air so he sailed across the first lane almost three feet off the ground. The car came right at him, the driver seeming to steer in his direction.

The van driver, seeing headlights abruptly veer into his lane, slammed on his brakes and tried to avoid the collision he already knew was about to happen.

The toboggan and Albert plunged from the air, pulled back to earth by gravity. However, the bank had done its job and he cleared the road to land on the other side, the sound of crunching metal and breaking glass filling the air a foot behind his head.

Landing, the toboggan continued onward, but only for a distance of four feet where it chose to stop rather suddenly in a deep bank of wind driven snow.

Rex arrived thirty seconds later, his tongue flapping from the right side of his mouth like a damp, deflated, pink balloon. He was out of breath yet thoroughly exhilarated. He hadn't had that much fun with the old man since ... well he didn't think he ever had.

Going around the wreckage of van and car, Rex tracked Albert to the snowdrift to find him slowly fighting his way out.

"*Hey, let's do that again!*" he nuzzled Albert's face.

Shocked that he was not only still alive but still had all his limbs intact, Albert marvelled at how few injuries he'd sustained. Admittedly, he was mostly frozen and questioned if one of his arms might just snap off if he moved it the wrong way, but nothing hurt and that was a miracle.

A muffled cry for help drew his attention to the car.

There were more headlights coming down the road now, a single set piercing the gloom from the direction of La Obrey.

Fastening his coat as best he could with completely numb fingers, he approached the car. The driver was dead, there was little chance he could be alive inside the crumpled mess the front end had become. But someone was in the back.

No, Albert realised as he got closer and saw the empty back seats, they were in the boot.

Tapping the boot lid with his knuckles, he called out, "Hello? Is there someone in there?"

"Albert?"

"Margot?"

"Yes!"

The how and why of her automobile incarceration could wait until he got her out, but freeing her when the keys or any release mechanism would be in the front presented a challenge.

Unseen by Albert, Lars raised his head. There was a gash just below his hairline from which blood flowed freely. His head pounded and he thought perhaps his right arm was dislocated. Acknowledging his need for medical attention, he nevertheless turned the key, trying to restart his stalled engine.

It cranked over but wouldn't catch. He couldn't see it, but the van's radiator was destroyed along with the front end of the engine where the alternator belt, coolant pump belt and a host of other important auxiliary functions were mounted. Even if he got it started, the van wasn't going anywhere.

Albert talked to Margot through the boot, holding his hands to his mouth to blow warmth into them and wishing the car coming their way would hurry up.

It cruised to a stop less than a minute later, the driver getting out to help.

"Oh, God, are you okay?" the man asked.

"I'm fine," Albert replied. "Just a little cold, but there's a woman stuck in the boot and I hope you have a tyre iron or something that we can use to pop this thing open."

He did indeed have a tyre iron, but while Albert was showing him the boot with Margot inside, Lars got into the driver's seat of the Samaritan's car, closed the door, and took off down the road. He'd rescued two bars of gold from the back of his van – all he could carry – and was bright enough to know he needed to leave while he still could. He might have killed the car's driver and Albert Smith had there not been cop cars streaming out of La Obrey. They were on the main road and coming his way. He left now or he went to jail. There was no chance to save the gold and jewels and he knew it.

Albert and the good Samaritan watched his car vanish into the distance, stunned looks on both their faces. They continued to watch it, neither man thinking of anything to say until a siren whooped and they turned to find a dozen cops all pointing their guns at Albert.

Chapter 56

It took Albert more than an hour to thaw out and warm up. According to the physician who checked him over, he hadn't been more than few minutes away from suffering hypothermia and was jolly lucky the frostbite on his hands, nose, and ears was superficial. Again, it would only have taken a few more minutes of exposure for the doctor to find he needed to start cutting parts off.

The police came to arrest Albert at the crash site, but the alibi Margot provided once they freed her, plus the confusion that followed finding their captain dead in the front seat of a car that wasn't his, proved enough to make them question everything.

When they subsequently found a stun gun in his pocket that Margot swore had been used to render her unconscious the real questions started. Then they found the gold, silver, and jewels in the back of the van and no one had so much as a working theory for where they had come from.

Not until the next morning when they found the hole in the treeline next to Drucker's Field.

Albert had to fight to stop them from taking him to hospital. He acknowledged that it might very well be necessary, but he refused to be separated from Rex and the paramedics were adamant his dog could not go with him. So they treated him in the back of their ambulance and returned him to his accommodation.

By the time he got back to the guesthouse, Celeste and Anton were long gone, both taken into custody. Anton would be tried for murder and undoubtedly be found guilty, but Celeste's fate was less certain.

Margot brought some supper since dinnertime came and went while he was in the back of the ambulance and Albert was in no mood nor physical shape to be going out anywhere.

They ate together in the two chairs in his room, talking over some of the elements of the case that had until now remained a mystery.

From Albert's report about Celeste, her son, and the conspiracy to keep Steve Cattrell's death a secret, Richard Allard, the sudden stand in chief of La Obrey police, went to see his grandfather. At eighty-nine and in very poor health, Charles Allard was relieved to get the truth off his chest. He confessed to burying Celeste's husband, assuring his grandson and the other cops present that he had rarely met a more loathsome human.

Margot explained all she had learned from her friends on the force – suddenly she was getting messages from everyone including the Allards, though not Curtis yet, and even from the ones who had never really bothered with her because she was a wet-behind-the-ears rookie.

Celeste stabbed her husband in a desperate attempt to save her son from a beating no one could possibly deserve. The wound didn't kill Steve right away though. With the knife sticking out of his chest, he fought back, striking Celeste with a clubbing blow that sent her flying down the stairs where she hit her head and fell unconscious.

Worried neighbours, unable to not hear the fighting and screaming coming from next door, ventured round to check all was well when they could hear the child wailing and no other sounds. They couldn't get into the locked house, so knocked for the man across the street, none other than a young police officer named Charles Allard.

Steve was dead and Celeste had lapsed into a coma so Charles, chose to manage justice his own way. It was all a terrible mess and the likelihood that Celeste would be found guilty of murder in an era when domestic abuse was yet to be recognised as a crime was simply too high. He couldn't allow it. If he reported the crime as he should, Celeste would go to jail and where was the justice in that?

He enlisted help, calling in favours from a couple of his good friends – Hugo from the café was one of them – and a small party of conspirators concocted the lie about Steve leaving in the night.

Celeste was in a coma for more than a year and when she returned her son was living contentedly with his 'new' mum and dad and a sister. Albert thought it must have been incredibly tough to choose to leave her son where he was, but also the most loving thing Celeste could have done in the circumstances.

There were others in the village who knew Celeste had been married, albeit only briefly, but as they died off and new people moved in, she became known as a spinster and no one fought to correct that belief.

When Rex bit Anton the first time, he limped home to rest and dress his wound, but unable to see to patch it properly, he called his 'aunt' who went to his aid. Albert surmised that Celeste must have dropped her blood-soaked handkerchief on the way home. Rex found it the next morning.

Celeste also darned the hole in Anton's coat, the excess thread getting caught on her sleeve where Albert found it. The police found a golf club at Anton's house with blood on it. That it would match Albert's was a dead certainty. They also found a pair of hopsack trousers with a chunk missing. They were in Anton's waste bin waiting for collection at the bottom of his drive.

Captain Allard was pronounced dead at the scene of the crash, but much like Celeste's crime so many years ago, it was being swept under the rug. He could not be charged and other than his stun gun attack on Margot, there was no crime to answer for.

The village would mourn him as the honourable law enforcer he was, at least that is what Margot believed would happen. Richard Allard, his eldest son and next most senior police office in La Obrey had already assumed the acting rank of captain and would most likely have his untimely promotion confirmed in the next week.

The mystery was solved, but the case was far from closed. There were press in the village already, though they were only local reporters. The bigger national tabloids and TV would show up soon enough and Albert was very much determined to not be around when they did.

He begged Margot to keep his name out of the story, but expected the press would figure out who the old Englishman with a German Shepherd was soon enough; there were too many people in the village who would make mention for it to go unrecorded.

What remained though was the mystery of the Swedish archaeologists and the Nazi gold. It hadn't taken much to realise that was what they were looking at, there were swastikas stamped into every bar as if that would somehow legitimise their plundering.

By the time Albert was ready to leave La Obrey on the afternoon after the mad downhill toboggan ride, the police had determined that Lars Nyqvist was not a member of the faculty at the Vasa Museum in Stockholm as he originally claimed and nor were any of his colleagues. So far as they could make out all four of the archaeological team were travelling under false IDs and no one believed they were ever looking for a Stone Age settlement. Not now.

They had somehow known there was a stash of Nazi plunder under the ground in Drucker's Field and were in La Obrey to find it. Maybe the police would track them down and maybe they wouldn't; Albert didn't really care. Margot told him a specialist team was on their way from Paris. They would handle the gold and other precious metals and gems recovered from the van and it would be they who investigated, not the cops in La Obrey.

Which was a good thing because the local cops had a case of their own to solve: the murder of Officer Marion Perrault.

The crime appeared devoid of motive, yet she was dead, and someone needed to answer for it.

Standing at the bus stop with the sun beginning to set, Albert knew it would be more sensible to stay another night in the village, but the press would find him if he did, so he chose to make good his escape. He would stay a night in Strasbourg, the biggest city in the Alsace region and in the morning would catch a train to take him out of France.

"Where are you going next?" Margot asked. She found that she felt rather melancholy. She met Albert just two days ago, but was sad to see him leave.

"Amsterdam," he replied, spying the bus coming down the road. "It's supposed to be quite picturesque. Also, they serve pancakes there and I rather fancy trying them to see if they are different to the ones I used to get at home."

Lifting his head, Rex said, *"Good plan. Let's go eat pancakes."*

The End.

Book 3 is waiting for you. Scan the QR code with your phone to find your copy of Old Fashioned.